The Revelation of Us

Labels & Lace

YD La Mar

Acknowledgments

To my wonderful husband, who never bats an eye when I come up with crazy ideas, but instead just adds to it, making my stories come alive. My children, who tell me every day that they are proud of me.

To my beta readers. You guys are the real MVP. Thank you for sticking with me through the initial phases of my writing journey. All of your feedback has inspired me to better myself and my writing ability. Anita, Alex, Dana, Vicky, Maria, **Tree**, Beth, Shaddy, **Kylie**, Gloria, Sasha, Kiki, and **everyone** who responded to my beta request in the dark group, and everyone else who beta read, thank you for bouncing ideas with me.

To all my readers, thank you for giving me the chance. I hope I can continue to make you guys proud.

Names

Fabian Hernandez

Nur Sakinah Binti Alqi

Hasanah

Hidaya

Mohd Akmal Bin Alqi

Veronica "Vero" Hernandez

Matunaagd Big Crow

Atsuko Kobayashi

Mohd Bisaam

Mohd Amir Bin Hafiz

Aunti Zunai (Amir's mother)

Jason Trafford

Omar Cortes

Translations

MALAY

Makan, Makan - Eat, Eat

Don't be perasan la - don't flatter yourself (la is sometimes added at the end of sentences)

Ibu, don't kacau him - mom, don't disturb him

Walao eh - Oh my god/oh shit

Can hah - Are you sure?

Bapa - dad

Ibu - mom

Cantik - beautiful/pretty

Anjing - dog

Jahanam - shit (distressful)

Aku sepak - I'll kick you

Apa kabar - how are you?

Nak pergi mana ke? - Where are you going?

———

SPANISH

¿Mira, mira quien viene? - Look, look who's coming

La bendición - asking for blessing, typical greeting

Que Dios te bendiga - God bless you, *reply* to La bendición

¿Tienes hambre? - are you hungry?

Comida - food

Cabrón - fucker

¿Quién es tu amigo/a? - Who is your friend?

¿Porque? - Why?

Mira tu boca! - Watch your mouth

¿Quién es tu novio/a? - who is your boyfriend/girlfriend?

Siéntate por favor - sit please

Esposo/esposa - husband/wife

Explícamelo - explain it to me

Hija/o - daughter/son

No te preocupes - don't you worry

¿Está embarazada? - is she pregnant?

Seria/serio - serious

Silencio - be quiet

Relájate - Relax

Dramatica - dramatic

Buen provecho - enjoy your meal

Mi cojones - my balls

una mujer - a woman

Ella es su novia - she's his girlfriend

Sin respeto - no respect

Blurb

Fabian Hernandez: The man who stole my first kiss.
My recently acquired brother in law.
From the moment he came into my life, he turned everything upside down.
There's a magnetism that keeps drawing us back together.
But we can't.
It isn't allowed.
It would bring shame.
It shouldn't have to be this hard, this complicated.
Maybe if I were someone else.
Someone without a controlling mother, a conservative culture.
A family and culture that sees this man as immediate family.
This is so difficult.
My hijab is getting too tight, everything around me is becoming too constricting.
Why must he drive me to the brink of madness with every touch, every kiss?
When things start to unravel, will I be strong enough to make the hardest decision of my life?

Courtesy Warning: This book may contain triggers for some. Triggers include but not limited to: violence, familial violence/abuse, subject matters that may be sensitive to some readers.

******* This book may contain authentic speech used by the different nationalities/ethnicities represented in this book. Some grammar usage was purposely done with broken English to continue to allow the story to flow authentically. ***

Author's Note

RECAP

Why is Fabian and Sakinah's potential relationship forbidden when they're technically not related? Well, an alpha reader [for the Malaysian side] has informed me that once you are married into the family, you are not allowed to have any sort of relations of that kind. It is not allowed and it is very much frowned upon.

What does this mean for our couple? It could mean many things. Middle sister Sakinah is the most rebellious of the girls in Akmal's family. She wishes to be more independent and westernized like Vero, as you see in this epilogue.

But you know what they say: be careful what you ask for because you just might get it.

This will lead to dramatic changes, ones she will have to learn to accept or she will have to learn to deny the love that grows between herself and Fabian.

Who would you choose? *Family or love?*

Chapter One

FABIAN

"Hey, what's up Omar."

This fucker and I have been working together at this construction site for the past five years. When we're on an off-season, we also do carpentry work as private contractors as well.

"Alrighty boys, let's get this shit done today." The boss is rounding up the guys now. It's been good working under Francisco. He's been fair and keeps it real.

We've been working on this building project for ages and can finally see the light at the end of the tunnel. It has been good and hard while it lasted, waking up at the crack of dawn consecutively. I'm actually looking forward to the little reprieve I'll be getting, to actually sleeping in. Shit, my dick is getting hard just thinking about it.

...the same way it does when...

The day goes by quickly. I almost made a few mistakes because of a certain Malaysian princess who seems to be taking over my mind these days.

Sakinah. The little minx that sasses as good as she slaps. For the life of me, I don't fucking understand why I'm so damn attracted to her. At thirty-six, I've been jumping from tail to tail. They come in droves when the boys and I are working the job. It also helps when the day's labor makes us hot, most of us start taking off our shirts to wipe the sweat off our faces.

Yet this girl, who's covered from damn head to toe in fabric, makes my blood boil hotter than a stripper on a pole. Shit, I need to get my head back into the game before I get myself killed on this construction site.

Yeah, I'm going to miss these days, but it's also good to take a break from this backbreaking shit. I'm probably aging faster by the second with how much I put my body through with these damn building projects in the city.

"Yo, Omar, where you headed after work?"

"Shit, this crap's got me so tired, I'm just going to go straight home, shower and crash. It's been a fucking week since I started getting a little pain in my knee."

"Yeah? You see a doctor for that shit?" Pot meet kettle. My body's been aching and creaking in new places too. I feel it more on cold mornings.

"I am now since the project is done." Fuck, the life of a construction worker. He's got that right. I wouldn't want a doctor's note to tell me I can't finish projects. That's too much money to pass up.

When the boss calls it for the day to end, the boys and I cheer.

"Job well done guys. Keep an ear out, I'll be calling everyone back in when we get a new contract." Everyone nods and starts to disperse, kicking up dust in their wake. Half the boys say they're going to hit up the bar after work, the other half are going wherever they usually go at the end of a work day. I usually hit up mi Mamá's casa for some homemade food since I'm too fucking tired after work to do any sort of cooking for myself.

Tossing my hard hat into the back of my 1970 Chevelle SS, I wipe my sweaty face one more time. I usually keep a few clean shirts in the back as well for hot days like this. I probably smell like a pig's balls, but at least a clean shirt will get me back home so I can take a cold shower. Moving the driver's seat forward to make room for my shoulders, I lean in and start rummaging through the shit in the back.

The sound of feminine giggles and gasps has me grabbing my shirt quickly and righting myself back up.

Standing about five feet away from me are some young ladies who look to be just coming back from the library downtown with how they're holding books in their hands.

"Ladies." It wouldn't do to be rude despite how they're checking out my naked torso. Scrunching up the grey T-shirt in my hand, I don't miss the gasps when I start putting it over my head.

"Hi." The brave one on the left says. They still haven't left despite not saying any more. Once I'm able to straighten out the shirt situation, I give them a smile and wink and push the driver's seat back to its original position and get in.

The Chevelle purrs before I throw it in gear and pull out of the parking structure. Rolling my windows down, the cool breeze refreshes me. My muscles are aching but it's a good ache. One that tells me I'll be getting a fat paycheck by the end of the week.

My mother still lives in our old dilapidated neighborhood and refuses to move despite the money I give her. Old habits I guess. It does get nostalgic every time I drive back home. The apartment I have closer to the city is probably collecting dust at this point since I barely go there. I should get rid of it and just save the damn cash. Maybe I should find something closer to mi Mamá's casa. She'd love that shit.

...Maybe I should find something near Sakinah. She'd hate that shit.

Throwing my car in park, I step out and start towards my mother's front door. Of course, she's been listening for my car's roar with her hands on her hips in her signature apron.

"La bendición." Girls might tell me I'm a bad boy but I'm really not. I know my manners and shit and never forget to ask my mother for blessings when I come home.

"Que Dios te bendiga. ¿Tienes hambre? I made a lot of comida because I know you eat like un caballo." Do I eat like a horse? I guess I do. I'm probably eating her out of house and home but she never tells me to leave, she just keeps feeding me more.

That's why I love mi Mamá. She takes care of me like that. I wonder if Sakinah would take care of me like that. I'm a simple guy, one that enjoys eating. Judging by the way Akmal's family serves food, I bet Sakinah can cook like a beast. Shit, thinking about her cooking for me makes my dick twitch.

The good thing about my mother's house is that she's never gotten rid of any of my stuff. Walking towards my old room, I grab a change of clothes before I hit up the modest single bathroom, leaving the door open in case anyone needs it while I'm in here.

The moment the cold water hits me, a shiver goes down my spine. It reminds me of Sakinah and how soft her damn lips are. The energy between us sizzles even though she refuses to acknowledge it. I've driven by her house a few times and notice that she doesn't always stay home. I wonder where she goes or if she lives somewhere else.

An image of that fucker at the wedding telling her how beautiful she is comes to mind and I want to punch the damn tiles. But I wouldn't do my parent's house like that, so I put an effort into holding myself back. Soaping myself up, I make sure to go over everything twice to get rid of all the sweat and dust I've attracted from the work-site. The sound of muffled footsteps makes me stop.

"Oye, Fabian, is that you?" My father always makes sure to use a louder voice when I'm in here.

"Si Papá. I'll be done in a minute." I don't hear what he says, but a few more swipes of soap all over my chest and between my legs, and I'm rinsing under the cold water. Sliding the glass door over I'm hit with the smell of...

"Papá, you need to warn me before you just up and take a shit while I'm in here!"

"A man can only do so much to control his bowels. What the hell am I supposed to do? Wait for you to get done washing tu culo? What if you take too long?"

My god, he knows I only take ten-minute showers. Wrapping my waist with a towel and grabbing another to cover my nose, I high tail it out of this confined room making sure to shut the door to have mercy on everyone else. He can kill someone with that smell. What the hell has he been eating?

Quickly getting dressed, I head into the kitchen to greet my mother again. Damn, at least the smell of her food is overpowering that shit I just walked through.

"Did you talk to tu hermana?" Vero's a married woman now, why would I be calling her? She's probably busy fucking her husband.

"No, she's probably making babies. I don't want to hear that shit." Grabbing a plate, something hits me in the back of my head hard. "Ow! Mamá!"

"Oi! Mira tu boca!" Turning my head, I see my mother putting her shoe back on. How does she do that shit so fast? Hispanic mothers must take some sort of class to master the chancla throw.

"You need to be making grandbabies for me. When are you going to find un mujer to bring home, huh? You're getting old."

"That's just mean, Mamá. I'm not that old."

"Too old." Am I? I don't feel like I am. Grabbing some tacos, I head to the table. Shit, if my mother thinks I'm old, what does Sakinah think of me?

Well, it fucking doesn't matter because it wouldn't stop me anyway.

Finishing up and putting the plate in the sink, I walk to the back to see if I need to grab any more spare shirts to keep in the car. I need to toss the dirty clothes into the laundry too while I'm here.

"Fabian, how's work going?"

"We just finished up our project. I'll be off for a good while until we get another contract."

"Yeah? Do you have any side jobs lined up?"

"Not yet. Omar is getting his knees checked out at the doctor's today. He said it's been acting up."

"Oh, that's too bad. If you guys need an extra hand, let me know hijo."

The sound of the front door opening makes us both turn.

"Alejandro, tu hija is home!" My mother's voice carries over into the laundry area. Vero's back? I wonder why.

"Vero! That was a beautiful wedding." I'm walking right behind my father when he suddenly stops in front of Vero. "What is wrong, Vero? Dónde está tu esposo?"

What the hell? Why does he sound so concerned like that? I can't see Vero's face too well since it's buried in my dad's chest in a bear hug. The hairs on the back of my neck are starting to rise. What the fuck did he do to her?

"Vero, what happened? Whose ass do I need to kick?" My eyes quickly dart to my mother in case a shoe comes flying but her expression tells me she's just as worried about Vero right now. I stand behind my dad just in case she changes her mind though.

"It's nothing guys. I just... I just need to clear my head a bit."

"Clear your head? What did Akmal do? Why are you guys fighting already?" Since when the fuck does my level headed sister need to clear her head? She's usually jumping into things head first but not without fore-thought. Well, I'm about to fucking find out for myself if I need to kick his ass or not.

My dad is taking Vero into the living room but I don't follow. Walking back into the laundry area for some privacy, I scroll through my phone for the only contact I have that's close enough to Akmal.

Bringing the phone to my ear, my mind starts to playback our last encounter at the wedding. It takes almost five rings before she decides to pick up. This girl and her ways of stringing me along. I've never been one to fall for that hard to get shit, but there's just something about Sakinah that tells me she doesn't play.

When she finally picks up, I'm annoyed the fuck out. How does this girl get the one up on me like this? I'm usually the one dragging women along.

"Hello?" The breathy sound of her voice makes my cock twitch. I miss the taste of her lips.

"Sakinah." All the shit I should say to her in my anger dissipates as thoughts of her body against mine start to take over. I'm an old horny bastard that probably should not be thinking of Akmal's sister this way. But how can I not with a voice like that?

My hand starts to rub over the jeans between my legs. She shouldn't affect me this way and not even physically be here to do anything about it.

"Hurry up, I got things I need to do." Fucking hell. I bet that pretty little mouth of hers would look good around my -

"Vero came home upset and shit. What did your brother do?"

"I don't know. He's not here with me, he's probably still at his apartment. Why don't you call him?"

"Because I only have your number, or did you forget when you slapped me and walked away?"

She doesn't say much else right before she fucking hangs up on me. I should leave a sassy little piece like that alone but damn if it doesn't make me want to find her and show her what she can do with that mouth of hers.

Leaving the laundry area in a slight daze I grill my sister about what's up. Sounds to me like a misunderstanding but the moment she tells me that Akmal told her to calm down... that boy just dug his own grave.

Every man should know this rule. Never - and I mean *never* - tell a woman to calm down. Especially a Puerto Rican Hernandez woman.

Sakinah was good on her word because not too long after Vero's dramatic entrance and moping around, I find Akmal coming up the front yard to fix the mess he made.

Giving him the advice he needs to hear, I watch as he mans up and takes his wife home. Watching them get into the car, something inside of me starts to feel funny. Though the screen door is closed, I wait and watch as Akmal takes my sister safely out of the neighborhood and back home where they belong. A breeze comes in bringing the smells of different types of food being made in this small neighborhood where houses are sometimes too close for comfort.

Where would I take Sakinah back to? My empty bachelor apartment near the city? Shit, I probably have bachelor written all over my face. It's no wonder she pushes me away and wants nothing to do with me. What can I do to convince her to give me a second look? Pressing my lips together, the memory of our kiss at the wedding comes back to me. She didn't seem that resistant to the idea of me then. It was actually getting pretty hot up until that slap.

Maybe I need a woman like her to keep me on my toes. All the women I've gone through are all the same. One and done, sometimes coming for seconds. But besides telling me how hot I am, they never want to stick around to even get to know me. And I never want them to stick around to show them who I am.

But Sakinah is basically family now. We'll be running into each other more often than not, right? Shit, maybe I should be running into her more to check up on her. Make sure that guy from the wedding isn't all up in her face while I'm over here eating tacos and watching my sister patch up her marriage.

At least she has something to patch up. What the fuck do I have?

Chapter Two

SAKINAH

Classes have been long and drawn out today. The thirteen credits I'm taking this semester aren't too bad. I'm usually going through things in a breeze. What is different this time?

Fabian.

Okay, you need to shut up brain. Fabian has nothing to do with anything. It probably has to do with the news about Vero and Atsuko's dual pregnancy. Yeah, that's got to be it. Walking to my last class of the day, Physics, my mind starts to wander towards the way Fabian pressed his lips to mine. He keeps stealing what doesn't belong to him...yet it was what every fantasy was made of.

I can't believe the asshole called me today saying we need to talk about what happened at the family lunch. It was going so well without thinking about him at all but the moment I heard his voice, my mind has been a jumbled mess.

We've been called back over to my parents house about something. I'm scared because I know Fabian's going to be there. How am I supposed to act around him? We're basically...kissing family members at this point.

My westernized brain is shouting that we're not blood related, but the Malaysian part of me is telling me we're committing the worst kind of taboo. If my parents ever found out...

Shaking my head, I continue to help Hasanah and Hidaya in the kitchen with the food.

About ten minutes afterwards, everyone starts coming in, but my eyes are already searching him out. Everyone does their greetings and Fabian is able to slip by unnoticed. My head is turned down as we walk a little away from the main crowd.

"Sakinah, I've missed you."

"You shouldn't say these things."

"Why?" I'm ticked he's putting me in this predicament, making my feelings bubble up again at the most inappropriate time.

"Fabian! We can't do this here!" I'm hissing under my breath as my eyes dart left and right in case anyone sees us talking a foot away from each other, pretending to mill about like everyone else.

"I can't stop thinking about you. About us."

"You need to!"

"Sakinah." When his hand tries to grab mine, I panic and jerk it away, turning and walking off towards the kitchen. He knows better than to follow me alone in this house. There are too many eyes looking. Too many eyes that might catch us.

"Aye, makan makan! Let's sit and eat. There is plenty of food!" My mother's voice carries all the way to where I'm hiding. Coming back into the living room, it seems there's already a pattern to the seating arrangement as we find our spots on the floor. Of course I have to be sitting next to Fabian. No matter how hard I try, it seems the universe keeps pushing us closer and closer together.

Fabian gives me a look and I shoot him a glare to tell him to behave. This can get ugly fast if any of my sisters catch us.

We're almost done eating in relative peace when my brother clears his throat. This must be what we're all here for.

"Everyone, Vero is pregnant!" Walao eh. Oh my god.

My eyes dart to Fabian's and he's looking at me intensely but not saying a word. Gathering up some of the dishes to put away and try to distract myself, I hear someone else announcing something. It's Atsuko.

"I have something to say too...I'm pregnant t-" I don't even wait for her to finish as I quickly gather plates with my sister and put them away in the kitchen. Hidaya is already

starting to wash them, so I excuse myself out the back door.

I need to concentrate on school and head back over there. I'm over halfway through my courses for this engineering major. Soon, soon I'll be able to start living life. My mother's been pushing me to find a husband but no one's been catching my eye.

Except -

I can't. We can't. The more I chant it into my mind the more my chest constricts. It's not fair. Malaysian culture can feel so oppressive sometimes. I wonder what it would be like to be like Vero who's comfortable in her own skin, who takes what she wants and gets her happy ending.

"Sakinah." Groaning, I start to question whether I'm just set up to fail.

"Fabian."

"What are you doing out here? Were you waiting for me?" This guy.

"Don't be perasan la. Don't flatter yourself, Fabian. Can't a girl just come out for some fresh air? Not everything revolves around you." I can't look at him right now. I turn to walk away only to be blocked in by his hard body a little ways away from the back door.

His front is to my back and my hands become locked in his grip as he brings them up to either side of my face, our fingers intertwined like the lovers we are not.

"What are you doing?" I don't mean to sound like I have an attitude but I am not feeling this crap right now.

"Sakinah. I can't stop thinking about you." My mind goes into a blur as we do this push and pull song and dance again.

When I'm finally able to escape him and the house, I drive myself all the way back to my place without looking in the rearview mirror.

"Ow, watch it." The masculine voice comes above my head as I'm already leaning down from dropping my stack of books. Damn engineering degrees with their ginormous textbooks. I used to wear it in my backpack, but then my back started hurting after a while.

"Oh! I'm so sorry!" Picking up my books from the ground, I stack them back together and start fast walking towards class. My gosh, Fabian needs to get out of my mind.

The roar of a familiar engine goes by but when I turn to look, there's nothing there. Nothing that would match the sound anyway. Ducking my head into the building doors, I make it to Physics with ten minutes to spare. I really should probably start leaving some of these books in my car.

"Hey! Sakinah, what are you going to do for the project?" Jason's turned around from the row below me.

"Oh! I don't know, I haven't thought that far just yet. Maybe something with velocity as a vector quantity."

"Yeah? Man, I don't know what I'm going to do." A cute little wrinkle forms on his forehead as he starts to scratch the back of his head. Jason and I have become a little bit closer than acquaintances since starting physics together. He's a nice white boy who usually greets me when I come in. He greets all the girls around him really, but isn't pushy beyond that.

A loud booming voice comes in and we all straighten in our seats as our professor makes his way towards his table.

"Alright ladies and gents, I've decided to make it a little easier on you guys and let you guys partner up for the project." Hoops and hollers can be heard all around me but I'm not joining in because not only do I have to think of the project details, now I have to find someone who would compliment the way I think. I don't want a partner who makes me do everything.

"Sakinah! Let's partner up! Please! I don't have any good ideas but I'm good at helping an idea that's already there. We'll be good together." Jason has his hands in a prayer position as he turns around to look at me again.

Ugh, I don't know what his work ethic is like, I never cared to know. But since we have to have partners, I might as well pick someone I can at least easily talk to, I guess.

"Yeah, we can partner up."

"Yes!" Jason is literally jumping up and down like a loon but since everyone around us is moving all over the place to look for partners, no one really notices him.

The professor let us use the rest of the time to get together with our groups and lay down ideas for our project that's due in two weeks time. Since Jason already inferred that we'll be using mine, we give ourselves a break today after exchanging necessary information.

"So how about we meet up at the library in two days at ...let's say 3 pm? How's your schedule looking?"

"My Wednesdays are usually short, yeah I can do that."

"Cool, see you then partner."

Waving him off, the professor announces the end of class. I really need to start putting these bricks of a textbook in the car.

Walking out through the front doors of the building, I'm trying my best to look down so I don't fall over the few steps down. Making it down alive, I almost released the breath I was holding only to run into something hard in front of me. But unlike last time, my books don't fall because the person is holding me by the arms with their strong arms.

"Oh, I'm so sorry! Man, why does this keep hap-" His cocky grin is the first thing I see and I already know who it belongs to. No one has a smile that can make panties melt like that on the science side of this damn campus. I know, I've looked...trying to find eye candy that could replace the image before me.

But no one does dreamy bad boy like Fabian Hernandez.

"What are you doing here Fabian?" Why my voice has so much attitude, I don't know. Just something about him that makes me put my guard up.

"Sakinah, why do you need to be like that? How about 'it's nice seeing you here' or something?" He's kidding right?

"I see you're here. What do you need?" Fabian laughs and my insides glow. It's a good thing my hijab is covering the flush that's probably showing on my skin. Those cute little crinkles by his eyes when he smiles like this makes me want to drop my books and just climb him like a tree.

Instead, I'm frowning at him and waiting for him to stop laughing and attracting all the attention from the females nearby. Ugh. Why does he have to have this kind of energy? Why the hell do I feel like I want to claw all these girls' eyes out? This makes my mood worse.

"Sakinah, you're much more beautiful when you smile, you know that? What's up with the frown? Here, let me help you with those books." What the hell am I supposed to say to that? I want to be mad, but I can't. Yanking my books away from him, I continue like I didn't just act like a petulant brat.

"Fabian, is there a reason why you are here?"

"Well, since you asked so nicely... I just so happened to be in the neighborhood and who do I see? The girl I've been thinking about all day." This asshole probably tells all the girl's this. I can feel my face scrunching at the thought.

"We've already established this Fabian. I don't think this friendship thing is going to work out."

"Sakinah, Sakinah, Sakinah. Why must you give up on us so easily? Come on, we can hang like adults and not make a thing about it, right?" What is he trying to say? That I'm not an adult?

"Look here, old man. I don't know what you're insinuating with your comment."

"Fucking hell, Sakinah. I want to hang out with you. That's what I'm *insinuating*. Can't a guy try his damndest to get a pretty girl by his side?" I can feel the butterflies fluttering inside my stomach, but I can't let it show. How can he just stand there in his stupid boots, form fitted jeans and button down shirt looking like a delicious snack talking about me being pretty? Vero and her brother are two of a kind in their vintage rockabilly looks.

Judging by the lingering females around us, I'm not the only one who thinks this way.

"I'm sure you have plenty of women lined up for the chance. Why don't you choose from your usual pool of females hmm?" I'm fishing, I know it. He better not agree or else I will kick his ass until next Tuesday. I'm staring daggers at him just daring him to say something about another woman.

"Damn Sakinah. There isn't anyone else and even if there was, which there *isn't*, it's not their company I'm seeking alright. I'm here aren't I? Do you see anyone else but us? No." I'm scared. I'm scared to get my hopes up for a man like Fabian.

A man who could very well take my offered heart and stomp all over it if he finds something better along the way. My head starts to feel tight under my hijab and my body is starting to heat up from the embarrassment I feel for something that hasn't even happened yet.

That's the problem though, right? *Yet.*

Turning around without another word, I start walking towards the student parking lot. I need to get out of here. How does Fabian make my emotions feel like I'm freefalling from a rollercoaster just by talking to me?

I can hear his boots following me and I start walking faster. It's juvenile, I know. But I can't help the way this fucker makes me feel like punching him and kissing him all at once! Is this how little boys feel when they're young and on the playground around someone they like?

My car is coming in sight and I'm almost about to sprint but I can't because of the dress I'm in today. My hand is already reaching into my pocket and fishing out the keys but before I can stick it in the door, I'm spun around and trapped by a whole lot of Fabian. Holding my books closer to my chest like it's a shield, my head tilts up to look at him with fire. If I didn't have these books in my arms, I would slap him in the face ... again.

Fabian is thinking the same thing because with both arms on either side of me, leaning against my little sedan, he comes closer in with a smirk.

"Sakinah." My eyes narrow.

"Fabian."

"Why are you being like this?"

"Like what?" Ugh, why *am* I like this?

"You should want to be around me. We're family after all."

"Yeah well, family shouldn't be asking each other out on dates then."

"Sakinah, go out with me. You might enjoy it more than you think...if you'd just let yourself."

"I'm busy that day." His laugh booms across the parking lot making even more girls stop. He needs to quit this shit. It's pissing me off.

"I haven't even decided on the date yet!"

"You don't have to. I'm busy."

Quicker than I can react, Fabian grabs my textbooks and puts them on top of the roof of my car right behind me, never letting me out of the cage of his arms.

"Sakinah."

"Fabian."

I'm about to open my mouth to tell him to fuck off somewhere else when his lips crash on mine again. This man...

This man's lips are so damn soft as he uses them expertly against mine and I can't help but fall prey to his wicked ways…

My god, Fabian is sin on a stick and I don't know how my arms ended up winding around his shoulders, pulling him into me even more. When he groans into my mouth as my breasts press against his chest, the spell of the moment gets broken. I nip his lip and push him as hard as my body will allow me.

Like the coward I am once more, I jump and grab my books before getting into the car and slamming the door shut. Letting out a long breath, I close my eyes but not before I lock the damn doors.

A thump startles me and has me looking out the side window to see Fabian rubbing his forehead on my car. This shouldn't look as endearing as it does. What is wrong with him? Why is he like this? His voice floats into the car slightly muffled.

"Sakinah, this isn't over." He straightens up and bores his eyes into mine, full of promises that make my nipples tighten. His intensity scares me. I don't know how to handle everything that is Fabian Hernandez, not like this. I don't know what I'm feeling, everything is so confusing. Even being the most rebellious sister didn't prepare me for a force of nature like him.

Waiting until he walks back to wherever he came from, I start the car and zoom out of the parking lot as fast as I can, careful not to run any of the other students over in my haste.

Chapter Three

FABIAN

This girl kills me. Fucking. Kills. Me. Why is it that everything that comes out of her damn mouth just makes my dick harder and harder? Fucking hell. I've run into plenty of sassy brats in my bachelorhood. I usually overlook these girls because life is too damn short to be chained to that kind of headache.

But Sakinah? Damn if my need for her doesn't just burn and come to fucking life when she pushes me away.

Like the pathetic fool I am, I've been following her around. Does that make me an old stalking bastard? So be it. That little spitfire lives in my fucking mind twenty-four-seven and I fucking hate it. I can't even kiss her to get her out of my system because she's slippery as hell.

But each taste she gives me only makes me more addicted - like a damn forbidden fruit. She's right of course, since we're basically family I probably shouldn't be asking her out but what hot blooded male in their right mind would let *that* woman slip through their fingertips without putting forth their best effort?

Shit, she only thinks this is all I got.

I switched out the car at my parent's house the moment I saw her on that damn campus while I was driving around. I'm following her car now because she's never seen me in anything other than my Chevelle. My car's roar is too distinct, she'd spot me a mile away. But with my parent's car, I can be right behind her - like I am right now - and she wouldn't have a clue.

She's been driving around aimlessly for the past thirty minutes. "What are you doing Sakinah?" Look at me, she's got me talking to myself while I'm on a mission to find out everything she does.

This is what happens when I have too much time on my hands. Watching her buy coffee and then drive back to the campus was torturous. She should've been kissing me, letting me touch her, letting me do things that will help keep her awake...then she wouldn't need no damn coffee.

My fingers hit the speed dial on my phone as we get closer and closer to the student parking lot at the side of the university.

"What's up? What do you need?" Damn, am I destined to be surrounded by sassy ass women or what?

"Vero, does Sakinah live on campus or what?"

"Why the hell do you want to know? Leave that girl alone if you're looking for someone to play with, alright? She's Akmal's sister. She's a good girl." Is she fucking hearing herself? Has she met Sakinah? *Good girl my ass.*

"Just answer the damn question."

"Puto, why should I be fucking involved in your shit? You know Akmal's culture doesn't allow for all that public affection and sexy shit before marriage. Sakinah has probably never even kissed before."

"Wait, hold up. Say that again?" This can't be real. I felt the way her lips pressed against mine. That kind of passion is not from a girl who hasn't kissed before. Vero has to be on something today.

"I fucking said what I fucking said. Sakinah and all of Akmal's sisters are innocent. That's why he's been so protective of them, not letting any of his classmates around the house. The girls are pure, Fabian. You probably don't know what that is." This perra right here, she better be fucking glad she's mi hermana. "If you ain't serious, leave her alone."

But that's the problem. All the shit Vero is telling me, just makes me dig my heels in deeper. I guessed Sakinah was inexperienced...but never been kissed? Nah. *No way.*

"You never answered the question Vero. She live on campus or what?" I can hear my sister let out an exasperated sigh. Shit, I probably called her in the middle of fucking her man or something with the attitude she's giving me.

"What the hell do I look like? Google? I don't know Fabian. Stop being weird." The entire time my sister is going off on me, Sakinah's car continues out the other end of the student parking lot and onto one of the smaller neighborhood streets. *Huh, what's this now? Where exactly are we headed?*

"Alright alright. Go back to your husband and tell him to put a leash on you. Sheesh."

"Pinche-" I don't need to hear that shit so I end the call. She can take out her frustrations with her husband. At least she has someone to take her frustrations out on. I haven't had sex in who knows how long with that recent contract taking up all my time and energy.

Well, I would have made time for Sakinah if she'd just let me in. But no...she had to be like *this*. She had to make me follow her ass around so I can get to know her and find better ways of convincing her to give me the time of day.

How did I become this?

When she pulls up into a modest little residence, my interest becomes piqued. Does she live here alone? I mean, it's better than on campus where there's other men around. But what if there are men next door and they take advantage of her because they know she's alone? My hands tighten on the steering wheel as I drive past her house and make another loop around to not look as suspicious.

This is going to have to be something we need to remedy. On my way back around, I pull the car into park right along the sidewalk and jump out. She's had at least five minutes to settle in so she shouldn't suspect me. Standing in front of her door, I try to look into her windows in case she's hiding someone in there. My mind is going a million miles a minute with the possibilities when I hear someone clearing their throat. Turning I see an older woman walking her little yapper dog, staring at me in disapproval.

Giving her a smile and a wave, I try to act like this is normal and knock on Sakinah's front door like I'm supposed to. The old woman needs to mind her own damn business any wa-

"Dammit Fabian! What. Do. You. Want?!" Aw hell, just look at her fire. *Fucking beautiful.* In fact, I'm so fucking turned on right now...

She tries to slam the door in my face but can't since I've already stuck my boot in the doorway. It is a good thing I tend to wear steel toes from working on construction sites. The door bangs loudly and practically vibrates as it jumps back with an equal amount of force.

Her eyes widen in the prettiest of ways and I just then realize that she doesn't have her headwrap on. *Holy shit.* I can't let this opportunity pass up, no way in hell.

I'm taking steps forward into her home and she starts to take tentative steps back. Closing and locking the door behind me, I turn back around and finally take her all in. *What the hell?* Is *this* how she walks around in her house?

What if there are weirdos out there trying to get a good look at what's mine?

Her shorts are hugging her ass deliciously and her tank top? Dios mio, her nipples are about to poke my eyes out with how hard they are. My mouth is fucking watering but I'm trying to stay strong.

Is this what she's been hiding under all that fabric? *Good.* It's what she should be hiding because hell if I'm going to fucking let her walk out in public like this.

"Stop looking at me like that. What the hell is your problem?"

"Look at you like what? Like you're the fucking sexiest woman I've ever seen? Like your body is making it hard for me to keep it in my fucking pants right now? Like I'm going to kill any motherfucker that even looks at you the way I do?"

She gasps and I swear it makes her tits bounce. She's doing this to me on purpose. She's poking the damn beast and right now I can barely walk straight with how hard I am behind my jeans. In fact, it's starting to ache, but seeing Sakinah like this is worth it. It's like being given a glimpse into something I'm not allowed to.

Does that make me a peeping whatever they call it? Nah, because she sees me looking right here and she isn't pushing me away. Oh no, in fact, I think there's desire in her pretty brown eyes right now despite the shit she spews at me.

I can feel my face grinning. I'm loving this game we play together. I don't even realize that I've been slowly walking towards her this entire time until she starts to bend over the back of her couch from being trapped. Well, I know for a damn fact she's good at slithering away when she wants to...does this mean, she wants this just like I do right now?

We're chest to chest and I can feel every breath she takes as her breasts press against my body, the warmth diffusing into my very senses as I continue to lean in as close as I can. Am I taking advantage of her? Nah, the hate she's throwing at me right now through her eyes tells me she can take care of her fucking self.

And I love that about her.

"Sakinah."

"Fabian." She's putting up a tough front but her voice is coming out breathier than when she answered the damn door earlier.

The sexual tension between us is practically sizzling the longer we both stand here just staring each other down. I know she feels it too even though she likes to deny it.

"How did you find me?"

"I followed you. Had to make sure my girl was alright. Wouldn't want any...predators to be chasing her around without her knowing. What kind of friend would that make me then, hmm?"

"We're not friends."

"Yeah? Then what are we?" My hands have slowly started creeping around her and between her shoulder blades. I can feel the tension radiating off her as my fingers continue to glide up until it threads through her beautiful fucking wavy hair that looks like it was made for a goddess.

Or a Malaysian princess.

Bringing my face closer to her, she shuts her eyes tightly like she's scared of what I'll do next. Haven't I shown her nothing but softness in my touches? Maybe I'm being a little too rough for this... what did my sister say about her?

"Sakinah and all of Akmal's sisters are innocent"

Vero's voice rings in my head but I still don't believe it. Sakinah's eyes are still glued shut like she's waiting for death but all I do is run the tip of my nose over her cheek, inhaling her scent. It's light and feminine, almost hidden just like her.

The longer I trail my nose all over her face, the more she starts to relax. *That's it, just let go.* Her lashes are so long and dark they sweep across her cheeks like the shit you only see in movies. When her eyes flutter open, I softly press my lips to hers so as to not scare her off. She's so skittish around me and thinks her little sassy personality can hide it. But when she's pliant like this in my arms, I know better.

Sakinah is afraid to let go.

I can be a patient man. I can be anything she needs me to be as long as she lets me in.

We both still have our eyes open as I give her another chaste kiss. I'm going to have to play this game differently with her. Find an opening and take it.

She finally turns her head away from me but still doesn't run. I think I'm wearing her down.

"Fabian, you fucking bastard. Why are you always stealing kisses from me?" Her voice has already lost its edge despite the words coming out of her mouth.

"Stealing? I don't know about that, Sakinah. Kind of seems like you welcome me in sometimes."

Her face turns back to me and her eyes are absolutely blazing. I'm about to lean in for another kiss when her hand cockblocks us by covering her mouth. *This girl.* Chuckling against her knuckles, I kiss them anyway.

She shoves me off with a hard push and moves herself quickly on the other side of the couch, creating an even bigger barrier between us. Jokes on her, as I cross my arms over my chest and concentrate my sights on those perky nipples that are still pushing against her tank top with every harsh breath she takes.

"I'll let that slide this time since I'm very much enjoying the view." With a cute shriek, she goes and has to ruin my day by crossing her own arms over her chest. Now we're a mirror image of each other. I wonder who has the ball in their court here?

"Look here..you...anjing! You've already stolen my first kiss. I forbid you from stealing anymore from me!" Holy mother of...

I'm staring at her intently. She's not telling the truth is she? This has to be another one of her games - trying to put me off her trail with shocking statements. Looking her up and down, the girl has to be in her early to mid twenties. First fucking kiss? ... and from a bastard like me?

I'd pat myself on the back if I knew it wouldn't piss her off more than she already apparently is. Well now, I think she just upped the stakes and I'm more than happy to take the challenge of being her other firsts.

Shit, did I think my cock was aching behind my pants before? Mi cojones are tightening just thinking about her beneath me, surrendering and moaning in pleasure. Shit, I can make her really happy if she'd let me.

"Well with that kind of information, I'm sure as hell glad it was me instead of some other asshole."

"Did you really just fucking say that?" I'm already starting to stalk her around the couch as she starts to pace around the opposite direction.

"Are you seriously thinking about kissing someone else? Because if you are, they're not going to be alive to find out. Sakinah, let's stop this nonsense. Get over here."

"Why should I? All you ever do is corner me."

"You make me."

"How so?" I jump over the couch and watch as she squeals and tries to run to the front door. The thing with little women is that they think they're going fast when in reality, each of my strides is probably equal to a few of theirs.

Grabbing her from the back, I lift her off her feet as she struggles and wriggles doing nothing but making my cock ache as her ass starts pressing into it. Burying my face into her hair, I groan. Damn this woman. She shouldn't feel this damn good in my arms even when she's fighting me like a she-demon.

Sniffing her again, my brain goes on overload with all this …. *Woman* in front of me.

"Sakinah, you smell so fucking delicio-" The knock on the front door makes us both freeze. "Sakinah, are you expecting company?"

She's panting, rubbing her tits on my arm with each breath as she shakes her head. Well then, it's a good thing I'm here in case this unexpected visit takes a turn. This is exactly why she shouldn't be here alone - this is exactly why I need to be following her around to make sure she's okay.

And now that I know what she wears when she's alone -

Shaking my head to dispel my thoughts, I walk towards the front door with Sakinah still in my arms. She's a small little thing and probably only weighs a bit over a hundred pounds soaking wet.

Shifting her weight to my left arm, I slowly put her feet on the ground without letting her go. She shifts and her ass presses right against my cock again.

"Dammit Sakinah, stop your wriggling. I'm going to end up busting a load right here before I can even open the damn door." Her intake of air is enough to let me know she'll behave for the next five minutes.

Swinging the door open I'm met with someone I don't recognize. Someone male.

"Yes, can I help you?" Luckily my smart brain told me not to open the door all the way but rather hide my delectable little Malaysian princess behind it. No one should be looking at her in what she's wearing or lack of anyway.

"I'm sorry, I thought -"

"You thought what?"

"I think I have the wrong house. Sorry about that." Is that so? This fucker looks Malaysian, so he probably has the right house but I'm not going to tell him that. In fact, once this guy leaves, I'm going to have a talk with my girl about having other men over when I'm not here.

"Tell me who you're looking for and I'll tell you if you got the wrong house. How about that?"

"Ah..she wouldn't be here. But I'm looking for Sakinah?"

"Yeah? That name kind of sounds familiar." Said woman is currently wriggling in my arms but my hand has automatically clasped over her beautiful lips right when this fucker opened his mouth.

He's looking at me funny. Yeah, I know. No normal guy would be struggling to stand just to answer a damn door. Get on with it bro.

"Oh? Do you know where she resides then? I was, uh, in the neighborhood and heard she lived near campus." Is that fucking right? What else does this guy know?

"Yeah? Well, I wouldn't know. My sister is married to her brother though, so you're probably better off asking him." At the suggestion the fucker starts to look a little sheepish. What is this then? I'm smelling something fishy.

"Ah, that's good. Well, if you see Akmal, tell him Amir came by and that we should catch up sometime."

"Sounds good."

"Alright. Thanks and sorry for interrupting anything. You have a good day."

"You too, man." Slamming the door before he could even turn to leave, I drag Sakinah towards the back of the house with my hand still over her mouth. Knowing her sassy ass, she'd probably yell or something just to get on my damn nerves.

Once we make it to what looks like a bedroom, I shut the door and let her go.

"What the hell are you doing!?"

"Why was there a guy looking for you Sakinah? You dating that fucker or something?"

"I have no damn idea what you're talking about. And so what if I am?" My head feels tight and my hands start to fist. Didn't she just fucking tell me I'm her first kiss. She better not be dating anyone. Not after all I've been doing just to get her to give me the damn time of day.

"You're not a cute liar, Sakinah."

"Fuck you. I'm not lying."

"Oh yeah? Guess I should go back out there and let him know you're taken then hmm? My fist is just itching to meet his face." Pretending to turn, Sakinah grabs onto me from behind. Trying to suppress a grin I know she can't see, I keep my body as still as I can. *I kind of like her giving me affection so willingly.*

"Who the hell is Amir and what is he doing here?"

"I don't know. He's one of Akmal's old classmates. My brother never lets any of them come over enough to get to know them."

"Is that right?" Turning around, I bend my knees a little and lift her by the ass so she can't run away from this conversation we're having so nicely. Sakinah's legs automatically wrap themselves around me as well as her arms to prevent her from feeling like she's falling.

Nuzzling into her neck, I breathe her delicate scent in. "So what is he doing here asking for my girl?"

"I'm not your girl." Her voice has become as soft as a whisper and it does something to me, more so than when she's all fire.

"You're not his either, so he shouldn't be here. He shouldn't know where you live - alone. He shouldn't fucking know where you're going to school either." Her skin is so damn soft and I can't help but run my nose along her collar bone.

"Are you talking about him or are you talking about yourself?"

"Oh, it's too damn late for you and I, Sakinah. You know this. This energy between us can't be ignored, no matter how much you try."

"...We can't" My lips brush over her neck as my tongue starts to lick at her skin, wanting just a taste.

Speaking against the crook of her neck, I'm confused. "Why not?" Oh, the little vixen seems like she's done playing because she's tilting her head back slightly, giving me more access.

Turning us around, I shove her back against the door in case she decides to try and slip away again. My lips are tracing her jaw when she turns her head away in an attempt to stop our connection.

"Fabian, we can't be together. We're family now."

"Not by blood, we're not." She starts to wriggle in earnest. Not wanting her to hurt herself, I let her body slide down against mine but keep her against the door, using my body as a blockade from any potential plans she might have brewing in that pretty head of hers.

She turns her eyes on me and it's a look I haven't seen on her before. It's almost ... vulnerable.

"Fabian. It's forbidden."

Lowering my voice to match hers, I ask the question that's burning inside of me. "Why?"

Her face turns into a snarl as she shoves at me passionately and I let her. This is a part of Sakinah I haven't seen before and it's taking me aback.

"Because Fabian! It's the damn same in my culture! It's like I'm telling everyone I've fallen in love with my brother, can't you see that? It's so easy for you to just..to just give into your feelings when I'm trapped! I can't have feelings for you! Not when I know it would just end in heartbreak."

Her voice cracks at the end and I just about tear my heart out of my chest. To see tough as nails Sakinah like this is something I don't want to see again. I'm at a loss for words, I mean, I've never been good with them to begin with - just ask my sister. She's cussing me out more times than not when we talk on the phone.

"I didn't know that."

"Of course you didn't! You're just being...Fabian! Too hot for your fucking self, strutting all over the damn place and making my fucking heart falter when I tell myself to get you the hell away from me!"

Make her heart falter? Does this mean she feels it too? About what we have between us? Life is so damn short, why are we letting this shit get between what's real? This shit. This shit right here, right now, is as real as it gets.

She's practically shaking with passion and rage at everything. Taking my own advice for once, I'm going to just shut up before I dig a bigger hole for myself. Grabbing her gently, I pull her back as I sit my ass down on the edge of her mattress. She doesn't offer any resistance as her body continues to tremble with everything she's just told me. Finally pulling her in the rest of the way, I let her fall into my arms and just hold her until the moment passes.

Chapter Four

SAKINAH

Why must he do this to me? Why must he drive me to the brink of madness and ...and hold me like this when I feel like my world is crashing down around me?

Did I really say all that? It came out like verbal vomit as my emotional threshold hit its maximum capabilities. My head feels hot, like a damn volcano just erupted taking casualties to those around me.

But Fabian - Fabian is still as strong as a rock and steady as the waters as he just holds me, rubbing my back in comfort. My arms are entwined around him, grabbing on like he's a damn life preserver as I drown in my emotions over the situation.

Fabian has come into my life and turned everything upside down. Even with all the rebellion I've thrown at my culture, he's the one I'm the scaredest to gamble on.

He has the potential to break my heart and confidence into a million pieces when he leaves. I just can't do that to myself, not when I've been trying so hard to become independent and strong and - be who I've always been meant to be. I don't know exactly what that is yet but it feels so close I can almost touch it.

When Fabian kisses the top of my head, my eyes tear up. My mind is warring with itself and neither side is gaining any momentum. Why must he be like this with me when it's so much easier to hate him when he's just being his cocky self?

"Fabian, please."

"Please what? What am I doing wrong?"

"You're just...too much."

"Sakinah, all I'm doing right now is comforting a friend. Can't we at least just be that right now?" I know I can be difficult. My brain is telling me that I'm leading him on when my heart says it wouldn't be so bad to be with a man who holds you when you can't stand on your own.

"Just friends then?" The cracks in my heart can practically be heard in my mind as I ask him this.

"Is that what you want?" I nod before I can think it through because as much as I push him, I don't want him to go.

He rearranges us until we're face to face, his hand caressing my cheek like I'm the most fragile thing he's ever held and it makes my heart want to burst.

"I'm going to be here for you, the way you want me to be Sakinah. But don't think I'm going to be happy about the fucking fact that other men are knocking on your door asking for you. Don't put me through that shit when I don't even get the fucking chance." It's not fair. It really isn't. Why life decided to throw this wrench at us, I'll never fucking understand it.

I don't regret gaining Vero as a sister, but I do regret making Fabian my family and off limits.

Pressing my forehead against his, I close my eyes because this is fucking heartbreaking. Can a person's heart hurt this bad before they even are allowed to give it away?

"I don't know what to do."

"I don't either. But I'm going to tell you right now, what I feel for you is real. I'mma step back as much as I can but I can't make any damn promises."

"We can't.."

"You said that already." Jumping out of his arms, I stand up and turn in irrational rage.

"It's not easy for me either! Just go, Fabian. I can't do this right now. Just go!" My tears start to fall as the sound of his footsteps and door slamming does exactly what I asked him to do.

———

It's been two days since Fabian crashed into my house. I'm almost scared to admit that I miss his stupid face.

The first half of the day went by in a blur, my mind still in a whirlwind about how I'm supposed to handle being 'friends' with the man who makes my insides and outsides tingle. This isn't going to work. I just know it. What did I get myself into?

"Sakinah!"

"Huh? Sorry, you were saying something?" Jason smirks my way from the seat in front of me and I realize the whole class is starting to clean up and leave. Damn, I don't remember a thing the professor even said.

"Yeah, I was saying it's Wednesday. Let's walk together to the library and hash this shit out. Get this project out the way quickly."

"Oh! Right, right. Yeah, okay." Bringing a backpack this time and leaving half my books in the car, the walk towards the next building wasn't riddled with me running into people since I can hold my head up.

The glass entrance to the library is wide and inviting. The sea of heads bent down on tables letting us know that there are people at work and to keep the noise level down. Jason picks a table towards the back end of the library and we both put our stuff down onto the chairs. There's only one other person back here so it shouldn't be too bad if our voices carry a little. Once we're seated, we drag the chairs on the carpet towards the round table.

"Okay, so what do you have? You said you already had an idea right? I'll just see where I should insert myself and we can start researching more from there."

"Okay." Having placed my backpack on the back of the chair, I turn around to unzip the compartment only to feel a displacement of cool air around me. Grabbing my folder, I straighten back out only to see another chair, turned backwards, placed between me and Jason. Fabian is sitting there with a smirk as he sticks his hands out towards my Physics partner.

What the hell is happening right now?

"Fabian. I'm Sakinah's friend. Figured I'd stop by and see what she was up to. You don't mind if I hang for a bit right? I was thinking of taking her out to lunch after this."

"Uh...nah, I guess not." Jason's eyes shoot to mine questioningly. I should be pissed at his audacity but in reality, I'm smiling on the inside about the fact that he's still forcefully inserting himself into my life.

I missed him. I shouldn't, but I did.

"Keep your damn voice down Fabian, we're in a library for crying out loud. Fabian, this is Jason. Jason, Fabian."

"Quit getting on me about everything, woman! I know it's a damn library for crying out loud. I have been in a few during my time, you know."

I hold back the laugh that wants to come out and Fabian narrows his eyes at me. Yeah, probably ten years ago.

"So.... You said your project was something on Velocity correct?" Jason's got a good memory.

"Yeah, velocity as a vector quantity." I'm pretty excited about it. Haven't thought of any sort of models to represent it yet though.

"That shit's way over my head Sakinah, maybe we should dumb it down a little."

"...Yeah Sakinah, help a dumb boy out." I elbow Fabian in the ribs even though Jason didn't hear him say it under his breath. How rude!

Opening my folder of notes, I try to find a way to explain it to him to see if he'll understand it better without having to change the whole project itself. Fabian leans into my side, crowding me as he looks over my pages too. This guy.

"Well...." Where do I start?

"It's like a beam moving in the air. If it goes one way and stays there, there's a velocity because it results in a change of position. But if your shit swings back, well ... then the motion just results in zero velocity because the thing practically comes back to its original position, that is until it swings back and knocks you off the building. Your shit shouldn't be swinging that hard to begin with."

My eyes widen as Fabian describes the situation to Jason. Jason is nodding his head trying to imagine the picture he just painted. Does Fabian work on building construction then? My eyes zoom in on his biceps flexing as he turns his head towards me and winks. My god, who is this man?

"But if you do need some housework done let me know. I got a few guys that can help out." Just imagining Fabian working with his hands is making me press my legs together.

"Um, thanks but we got it from here. Maybe you should wait for me in the car? We won't be too much longer since we're just laying the ideas out, right Jason?" Jason is looking between us back and forth probably wondering what's really going on but nods his head.

"Yeah, we'll just handle an outline today and meet again to see what kind of model we want to make to represent it."

"I'm sitting my ass right here. I don't mind waiting, Sakinah. Don't fret your pretty head over me for my sake." The stubborn bastard. I'm trying hard to be civil and not rip his head off because we have company and he knows it judging by the smirk he's giving me.

"Well, then scoot over there so I can show Jason my notes."

"Nah, I'm fine right here. Jason can see that shit from where he's sitting, right Jason?"

He's looking between us again, the tension in the room starting to amp up. "Right..."

"In fact, I don't mind passing the notes. How about this, Sakinah will make you a copy and I'll make sure to hand it to ya tomorrow? Sakinah, we don't want to be late for our lunch. She studies too much. Need to keep on her check before she starves herself."

"Yeah? Yeah, of course." Jason gets up and starts packing. My eyes are boring into the back of Fabian's skull but he doesn't notice because he's watching Jason's every move, making sure he really leaves.

Once Jason is halfway towards the front of the library, I hit Fabian with the back of my hand on his shoulder. "Oi Fabian! You can't just barge in and cut my project meetings short! This is an important assignment."

"Yeah, I figured that, which is why I'm going to hand lover boy over there a copy of your damn notes so he doesn't waste any more of your time pretending to listen while he's really looking at your tits." What the hell?

"What the hell are you talking about?"

"Come on Sakinah, you can't be that dense. As a *friend*, I need to make you aware of how you affect the opposite sex. After all, I would know." Fabian takes that very moment to blatantly stare at my tits and I become self-conscious, covering it up with the backpack I just removed from the back of my chair after packing it back up.

I should have never worn this long sleeve shirt. I thought my hijab was doing a good job covering the neckline. Fabian startles me when he grabs the backpack off my hands and throws it over his shoulder. I'm standing there stunned by his actions when he grabs my hand firmly and starts walking us towards the front of the library, towards the exit.

"You need to know by now that men don't need the hint of actual flesh to visualize what's underneath. He'll probably be jacking off to fantasies of your tits in his face tonight, I guarantee it."

"Fabian!"

"Shhhh! This is a library Miss!"

"Sorry!"

"Yeah Sakinah, keep it down. This is a library for crying out loud." Another round of shushes follow us as we exit out the double doors making me stifle a laugh. This troublemaker is going to get me kicked out of the damn library, then where would I go for projects?

My short legs are struggling to catch up with him as I almost trip over nothing. Fabian turns around abruptly and throws me over his damn shoulder, continuing on our course like it's just another day.

"Fabian! Put me down! How fucking embarrassing! I can walk!"

"Yeah, well you're taking too damn long and I'm fucking starving. All that talk of physics and beams knocking you over the side of a building builds an appetite." He slaps my ass after one of my kicks hits him in his hard abs. This guy is like a damn brick house and his muscles don't help my stomach when he's bouncing me over his shoulder.

I almost fall backward when he throws me off his shoulder and back into standing if it wasn't for his arms holding me against his chest. Rubbing my head against him, I try to get my dizziness back in order before glaring at his stupid cocky face.

"Better? Now let's go." The sound of a metal car door opens and he's shoving me into his Chevelle. The only reason I know this is because I was scouring google the moment he left my parent's house after that first meeting. That doesn't make me obsessed though, I was just trying to get information, that's all.

The door slams, reminding me of a damn tin can for some reason as I watch Fabian round the car to the driver's side. "Alright, put on your seat belt, we're going on a friendly lunch." My eyes playfully look at his as I do what he says. Friendly lunch huh, I think he just wrangled himself a date.

Surprisingly for a stick shift, the car ride over was a smooth one. I had to try my best to keep my eyes forward so as to not let him know that I'm checking out the way his forearm flexes every time he shifts. Knowing what I know now - Fabian being a man who works with his body - my mind is now trying to imagine what's under his shirt.

He pulls up into what looks like a taco shop near the campus. How does he even know this is here anyway? Doesn't Fabian live in a whole other town?

"Fabian.."

"I scouted it out. Keep your sassy comments to yourself. Just go in and eat with me, enjoy the damn time. I want to hang out with my friend, is that so bad?"

Blinking a few times, I'm starting to wonder if he can read minds. I'm also starting to look at him from a different light. From his talk of physics to this, Fabian Hernandez is not the stereotypical bad boy I thought he was. I mean, he still reeks of trouble but something about what he's shown me is making my insides melt a little.

Despite the fact that he just kind of admitted to stalking my stomping grounds. *That should be creepy.*

Watching Fabian come around to open the passenger door for me, I can't help but tell my brain to shut up as I place my hand in his so he can help me out of the car. His smile makes me blush but I look down and clear my throat to get his eyes off me.

"So tacos, huh?"

"Best place to take a friend, I say. Plus I'm starving as hell." I laugh as he leads me to the front door and opens it for me. Such a gentleman under his cocky exterior. Guess his mama taught him well.

We sit down and I swear Fabian is ordering half the menu. The server is batting her eyelashes a little too much and smiling a bit too long. It makes me want to sharpen my metaphorical claws. Crossing my arms, I clear my throat to get her attention. I can see Fabian smirking at me from my periphery as I ask her what their specials are.

"Just give her a plate of chicken tacos. She can share some of mine if she wants to try something out. Thanks."

"I could order for myself, you know."

"Yeah, but I ordered for you so I won't starve to fucking death waiting for you to make up your damn mind."

"You're such a…"

"Great guy, that was kind enough to order for you so you don't have to look like you don't know what you're doing? You're welcome. That's what I'm here for." Suppressing a smile, I look down at the table as Fabian's masculine chuckle comes from across the table.

"What do you like to do Sakinah? Being friends, we should be getting to know one another."

"I like..science? And engineering. That's what I'm going for. I'm hoping to be able to break away from the family work and just do something for myself, you know?"

"Yeah? You seem good at it." I automatically beam at his praise. My mother used to complain that I'm taking the long way when I could have majored in something else that would spit me out of school faster so I can find a husband and make a million babies for her.

Looking at Fabian and his free spirit, I find myself a bit envious but I swallow it down as the waitress comes back with a few cups of water for us.

"What do you do Fabian?" After a few large gulps that make my eyes zero in on how his Adam's apple bobs, he set's the cup down.

"I work whatever I can. Usually, when the site has a contract, I'll have work for months on end, maybe even years. But between the contracts, I'm basically a private contractor for myself, selling my skills to whoever needs it." I love the fact that Fabian says everything so confidently like it's just a part of who he is. I want this kind of energy, this kind of confidence.

The food arrives and we eat in relative silence. Well, I eat while I watch Fabian inhale about five plates of food in front of my very eyes. Holy shit. Knowing what I know now about him and manual labor, I can see why he would be so damn hungry - he has to keep his energy up.

The ... friendly lunch is over before I know it and we're back in his car, driving around aimlessly. Doesn't this thing burn gas?

"Don't you live another town over?"

"Yeah."

"So why are you all the way over here?"

"Let's not play this game Sakinah. You know I'm over here for you. I'm watching out for you. The moment I found out you're living alone is the moment I started coming by to make sure you're alright. Your parents should have never left you here like this. At least get you a damn roommate. Even that's iffy."

"What the hell do you mean, my parents should have never let me? I'm a fucking adult, why should they dictate where I go? I needed to be near my campus."

Fabian laughs. Fucking laughs! What the hell is so funny right now?

"Keep your claws in, alright? All I'm saying is that a pretty woman shouldn't be left on her own in a neighborhood that might be filled with predators."

"Oh, like you?" We're stopped at a red light and Fabian turns his face to me with a look I can't decipher.

"Yeah, fucking like me. But unlike me, they don't have your best interest at heart, ya feel? Because we're fucking family *as you say*, and I take care of family. I'm not letting other guys come over thinking they can take advantage of you."

I'm pissed but at the same time flattered. He always does this to me, leaving me without a good retort back. By the time I'm about to come up with something to say, the moment's already passed and he's parking in front of my little place behind campus.

"Come on, I'm going to see you inside. That way any neighbor thinking of trying anything will think twice." With the rolled-up sleeves on his t-shirt letting his tattoos peek out to the chain hanging down his front to his back pocket, I don't think any of the students who live near me would dare to do anything.

He walks me up to the front door like a damn proper date and my skin is prickling with awareness. We're both lying to each other right now with this friendship thing, and we both know it. Isn't this where the boy kisses the girls? I'm nervous and I don't know why.

Unlocking the door, I can feel Fabian's body heat right behind me, blocking me from anyone on the street that might walk by. He makes me feel protected but I'm not going to tell him that because it would just solidify everything he's been spewing in the car. Opening the door and stepping through, I turn to find Fabian with both of his arms on each side of the doorway, leaning in.

"Well, thank you. For lunch." Why am I so embarrassed all of a sudden? My face feels like it's flaming and it's getting hot under my long sleeve.

"Of course."

We both stand there awkwardly, unsure of how this friend thing is supposed to work, how far we're allowed to go. *You did this to yourself, you know.*

"Sakinah." When did I start staring at the floor? Lifting my eyes to his, I don't have time to prepare for him to barge in again, grabbing my face and kissing me so softly that I want to cry. Why am I so damn emotional?

He must have kicked the door shut with his boots because he doesn't take his lips off mine until we're against the back of the couch once more.

Is this Deja vu or what?

His tongue teases the slit between my lips and I'm lost in the moment of wanting something so badly, something I can never have. Inviting him in, our kiss turns passionate and frenzied until I'm left there standing with my lips parted as Fabian sees himself out, slamming the door.

Chapter Five

SAKINAH

Fabian was good on his word and gave Jason a copy of my notes. I'm assuming so anyway since Jason didn't ask me for it when I saw him in class the next day. All we talked about was whether our library meeting was still happening tomorrow.

My mother called me back home for something and since one of my later classes got canceled, I decided to head over there around lunch. I wonder what this is about since Hasanah and Hidaya are still around the house to help out if she needs it.

Pulling up my sedan to the front of the house, Ibu is already standing out there at the doorway. Damn, how long has she been waiting? Getting out of the driver's side, I try to put a polite smile on my face.

"Ibu! I hope you haven't been standing there long."

"Sakinah! Come on, come inside. Your sisters are already in the kitchen." Okay...

Once I make it inside my childhood home, the smells of different food cooking make my stomach growl. I haven't eaten yet so this is perfect. My sisters and I start setting up plates in the living room and I swear it looks like way too much food for just us -

"Ahh, come in, come in. Food is done, there is plenty to eat!" My mother's voice is loud and clear from the front door and my sisters and I look at each other in confusion.

"Who's coming?"

"I don't know." Hidaya just shrugs her shoulders when I look over to her.

When the voices get closer, Hasanah and I look at each other again with knowing glances. *Oh no.* Ibu is trying to set us up again.

"Bisaam, Amir, please sit down."

Hasanah and I nervously say our greetings as we start to sit on the floor. My father isn't home right now so it's just us girls as we all sit in a circle.

"Hasanah! This is Bisaam, he comes from a great family. You remember him huh? He is Akmal's classmate. So is Amir. You remember Aunti Zunai? This is her son."

Hisanah and I are trying not to laugh and groan at the same time. Ibu always does this. I mean she's stopped for a while since I started university but has never stopped hinting at us finding a husband.

"Bisaam! Doesn't Hasanah look beautiful? She helps me around the house the most la. Amir! You asked me about Sakinah at Akmal's wedding. Did you know my daughter studies at the university? Engineering la. Very smart girl, very smart."

"Yes, Ibu." Hasanah and I have been through this before. But Ibu has never been this pushy.

"Bisaam and Amir will make very good husbands, their families have very good business. Hasanah and Sakinah are very good wives too, they learn from the best huh?"

We all laugh nervously together at this makeshift match-making auction. Gosh, Malay culture can be a trip. How do I get myself out of this? Wasn't Amir at my house the other day? How did he even know where I live? My eyes narrow a bit when I look at him. He catches my eye and just gives me a soft smile.

He looks like the typical Malay man. Clean, hair combed back -

"They come from good families. You would be proud to have these men as husbands." Walao eh - Oh my god. Can my mother be any more embarrassing right now? When I look over to Hasanah, I noticed that both she and Bisaam are making googly eyes at each other.

There has to be a story here. They must have already expressed interest in one another. No way, homebody Hasanah, would just quickly like someone on the first day.

Turning my head to look at Amir, I can't find myself feeling the same sentiment. His eyes are soft as they look at mine, the way Fabian sometimes looks when he lets his guard down. But ... he's no Fabian. I can't help but compare them even though I know I shouldn't.

"I'm going to go to the kitchen for something huh, you guys talk. Makan, makan. Ooo, Sakinah! You and Amir look so good together! Talk, talk, I'm going to the kitchen huh." My mother is so *not* slick with her blatant interest in us all hooking up like some damn dating show. She's probably going to be peeping from the other room, eavesdropping on everything that's said. Poor Hidaya looks like a third wheel, just trying to stuff her face so she doesn't feel awkward right now. My mother comes over to me and I'm anticipating something weird, which I should because she starts to fix my hijab like she's prepping a show dog before heading back into the kitchen.

"Sakinah, apa kabar? How are you?" Amir is almost leaning into me as I lean back.

"I'm fine, thanks." My mother flutters back with another plate of something while she takes some of the half-empty plates back into the kitchen. *So freaking weird aye.*

"How's the university? I came by the other day but I think I got the wrong house?" *How does he even know where I live anyway?* I side-eye my mother who's hiding behind one of the pillars in the kitchen, pretending to put some plates back into the cabinet. *I bet she pushed him my way.*

"Oh?"

"Yeah, some Hispanic guy answered the door. I was sure I was at the right house too."

"Oh, yeah. That was just a friend. He was watching my house for me when I was in class. I needed something fixed inside the house." Sounds legit, right?

"Yeah? Hey, look. If you'd like to go out sometime -"

"Sorry, Amir. I don't think so."

"Yeah? But your mother-"

"Yeah, she can be a bit pushy, you know?" My mother's booming laugh comes from the kitchen and I jump from getting startled. I think she's laughing at something Hasanah and Bisaam are talking about. What a creep aye.

"Um, excuse me for a minute..."

"Nak pergi mana ke? Where are you going?" Far away from you and from my Ibu who is scolding me with her hand gestures from the kitchen. Aduh, my god this is too much. My head is practically pounding from this stupid luncheon. I didn't even get to eat everything since my mother practically shoved these guys down our throats wanting to be matchmaker.

My mother grabs me by the arm and literally drags me back into the living room towards our male guests again.

"Haiya Sakinah, why don't you show Amir around the neighborhood, hmm? I'm sure you'll get to know each other better after spending some time together." Ibu claps her hands together in excitement, almost like a little kid. What is going on here? Who is the one getting matched?

I swear my mother acts like it's *her* getting a new husband.

"If you like him so much, why don't you marry him huh?" I'm whisper-hissing at my mother and she just shakes me with a stern look. I can't stand this shit. I need to get out of here. I feel stifled, pressed down. This can't be what my life is all about. My mother throwing the 'perfect Malay' guy at me - a guy I'm not even attracted to whatsoever.

"Sakinah, you need to do the right thing and start looking for a husband. You are getting old!" She did not just say that to me. I'm only twenty-five! She's acting like my eggs are drying up before her very eyes.

"I'm getting old la! I need some grandbabies. Akmal is at least working on it. How about you huh? What are you doing? You are watching me get old and die before you even find a man."

"Ibu! Why are you so dramatic!?" She pinches my tummy and dramatically responds like a damn soap opera.

"You are getting old! Then you will not look as pretty anymore to catch a good man. You need a husband now before it's too late!" Her voice raises in octaves towards the end and everyone in the living room shuts up as she screams to the world that I'm going to get too old and decrepit by tomorrow, therefore will not be able to find anyone to take me as a wife.

I want to die. Why is she like this? I'm looking around thinking there has to be some sort of prank cameras set up because this is straight out of the Malaysian soap operas she watches.

"Your aunty is only 45 and she just became a grandma. When is my turn?" *My god.*

"Ibu! You'll have Akmal's baby soon!"

My mother temporarily gives up on me because of my sheer stubbornness in this and starts to flutter around Hasanah who is preening like a damn peacock. Hasanah is older than I am, she's also expressed her hopeless romantic notions of finding love soon. I'm happy for her if she's showing interest in Bisaam. He seems like a nice guy who looks like he's really into her as well.

While my mother is ooh-ing and aah-ing over the potential match, I slip out the backdoor and run to my car to make my escape. I've only just started the car when I hear my Ibu's voice yelling in the wind.

"Sakinah! Where are you going? What are you doing? When are you coming back huh?"

I put the gear in drive and step on the gas like the cops are after me. I guess I'll have to get lunch when I get home.

The drive back to my residence was a calming one. With soothing music in the car, I let the windows down and just take in a breath of fresh air. I don't know how long I'll be able to avoid my mother with her plans on matchmaking.

My neighborhood comes into view and the sight of the campus starts to release some of the tension I've been holding in from my escape. Who knew the sight of the place where professors torture your mind would be relieving?

Pulling up to my tiny one-car garage, I park the car and my mind drifts to Fabian again. There's no competition. If Amir were to stand side by side with Fabian...

Shaking my head, I tell myself I can't think this way because it'll never happen. Grabbing my bag out of my car, I rip off my hijab and inner cap in frustration and shake my hair out. What would it be like to be a normal westernized girl with no restrictions? To not have the confinements of a culture that literally feels like it's pressing you down into the ground - and then presses you down even more with situations like the one my mother loves to put me in.

Slamming my car door in frustration, I remind myself once more to stop thinking along those lines because this is who I am, this is the family and life I was born into. I can't change a damn thing about it. I'm rummaging through my purse for my keys, walking up my steps when I run into a hard body. Dammit! I'm about to cry with how frustrating this lunch went. I'm so damn *hangry* that I can't think straight but when I lift my head I feel like a weight has been lifted off my shoulders.

Fabian's here with what looks like a bag of food in his hand.

"Fabian." His name on my lips comes out almost like a sigh of relief.

I throw caution into the wind and just hug him. All of the day's activities are catching up to me and I don't know who to talk to. I used to be able to talk to my sisters about it, but with the way Hasanah was looking at Bisaam, I think that boat has sailed for me. I no longer have an ally on my side in these marriage matters. Well, except for Hidaya, but it's not the same - the trio is breaking up.

"What's wrong?"

Burying my face even deeper into his chest, I just shove my keys at him. Fabian didn't need more instruction than that as he unlocks the door and drags us both inside without separating our embrace.

I hear the door shut before I feel him pick me up bridal style while still holding onto the bag of food and sitting us on the couch. He leans over carefully to place the bag on the coffee table before sitting back and just rubbing my back. *How does he always know what I need?*

We're both quiet as Fabian rubs my back until I'm ready to sit up. A few minutes go by and we both start taking food out of the paper bag Fabian brought over and eat in silence. It's a dramatic contrast to what I just left at home, a house full of bickering over when the hypothetical wedding should be - even if my mother didn't say it out loud just yet - and when I'll be making babies.

Fabian brought over some burgers and fries and my chest feels full with what he's done for me in a time of need without having to be told.

"Thank you."

"Of course. I gotta feed my girl. We're friends after all."

The term always stabs me in the chest when I think about it. A double-edged sword that I pointed at myself. When we're done eating, I get up to throw the trash away and Fabian follows me into the kitchen. It's quiet and there's a subtle tension and energy simmering between us but neither of us wants to point it out. I'm backed against the kitchen counter while Fabian cages me in again, but this time...this time it feels comforting rather than intimidating.

We're staring at each other and I swear I can feel the electricity pulsing, pulling us closer. How can we possibly even try this friendship thing when it's always like this between us?

Fabian leans in and I find myself closing my eyes, surrendering to the moment when right before his lips touch mine, there's a knock on the door. Groaning right before he gives me a chaste kiss anyway, Fabian turns to go answer the door like he lives here.

"Yes?"

"I'm looking for Sakinah. I'm guessing she's not home because you're here. She told me that you help watch her house for her."

"Is that right?" I swallow a lump in my throat, afraid of Fabian getting offended because I didn't get to explain to him what happened at my mother's house. *Oh god, I don't even want to see how he would react to that.* My face feels hot from embarrassment and my scalp is getting tingles from what Fabian might do right now. Is he going to tell Amir I'm home?

"Yeah, so when she comes back, will you let her know that uh...I was serious about what we were talking about." Fabian's back tenses up but he doesn't move his position in front of the door - the door that's only opened halfway while I'm hiding in the kitchen once more like a coward.

"I'll make sure to ... let her know. Though it'll be hard to tell her a clear message if I don't know what the message actually is. What did you say you guys talked about again?"

"Ah..well, tell her I'll come by tomorrow to pick her up. Say around seven. Alright, thanks for giving her my message man. I'll text her later as well."

Fabian literally slams the door in Amir's face before he turns those blazing orbs at me. I feel like shrinking into myself, my hands are clasped before me.

"I-I"

"Where were you today?"

"I-I was at my mother's house. She asked me to come over and-and-"

"And what Sakinah? Why is this guy here saying he's coming by tomorrow to pick you up? For fucking what? A date? What the hell is he talking about with this 'what we were talking about' shit? Were you with him today Sakinah?"

"Fabian! It's not like that! My mother was trying to be a matchmaker again!"

"So you're saying you're supposed to marry this fucker?"

"Dammit, Fabian! I'm trying to tell you! Just listen!"

"Did I not just hear that fucker standing at *your* damn door talking about picking *you* up tomorrow for a fucking *date* at seven? I heard every. Damn. Word." I can feel the burn behind my eyes from the tears that want to come out but I'm so pissed I just want to throw something at his stubborn ass head. Why isn't he listening to me?!

"Fabian! I didn't agree to anything! That's why I came home fucking hungry. I left before it could go any further. It's not my fault my mother wants to marry all her daughters off. It's not my damn fault she invited him over to trap me!"

Fabian rubs his hand down his face and is starting to pace around the living room. I don't know what to do, I don't know how to feel. I'm embarrassed, I'm scared, I'm mad - I feel like I'm suffocating right now and I don't even have my hijab on.

After wearing my carpet down with his boots, I watch as Fabian starts running his hands through his hair right before he turns towards me again. The anger in his eyes has lessened but there's still something else there that makes my stomach churn.

"So you were put into a predicament and yet...yet you couldn't even tell him I was a friend? I'm reduced to some guy that what? Watches the house for you? That's pretty fucking messed up Sakinah."

"I-I-I didn't know how to explain what happened last time! It just came out like that."

"Yeah? It just came out like that...like what? Because I'm too beneath you to be called anything else?" Fabian turns again, punches the back of the couch and storms out the front door, slamming it shut as I fall to my knees in this stupid kitchen I thought would protect me from this tornado of emotions.

Chapter Six

FABIAN

I parked a couple of blocks away because I didn't want her to hear the roar of my engine when I came over. I wanted it to be a surprise because friends do that, right? Just a nice little lunch to help pick up her spirits or whatever.

I'm fucking glad I parked far because I need to cool my head right now with everything that just went down. My head feels tight, like it's about to explode and no matter how many times I run my hand through my hair, it doesn't fucking help to ease the tension that's building.

The cool breeze cools my ardor only a little bit while my mind is still racing with all the information that was just thrown at me like a damn hand grenade. Her mother wants her married and she brought a damn candidate over.

Fucker comes to Sakinah's house and just throws down the gauntlet in front of my damn face with that date shit. I saw the way he was looking at me because I was looking at him in the same damn way.

Walking around the back of my car, I open the driver's side and slide in, slamming the door harder than I should. This neighborhood is quiet. After scouting it out a few times, I haven't seen many troublemakers about. It was another reason why I came by with lunch - I recently ended my lease for my apartment near the city. What better place to look than to be near the woman that haunts me every damn waking moment.

Pulling out onto the street my mind starts to whir with different scenarios between us, none of which involves that fucker at her door. Am I so bad that she couldn't even stand up for me in front of him at her mother's house? I mean, I'm fucking family after all, she could have said *that*.

About halfway out of her neighborhood, I turn around the front of the campus when my mind finally gives me the answers. Well, part of the answers I'm looking for. Sakinah thinks our closeness is a forbidden taboo. Could this be why she couldn't tell anyone why I was there? But if that's the case, what the hell does that make me? A hidden secret? *A dirty secret.* My skin itches with just the thought of that. I don't want to be anyone's fucking dirty secret.

I think it's time for Sakinah to start making up her mind about what she's going to do. With this Amir guy in the picture, it's only going to make her even more confused. Yeah, he'll be there tomorrow at seven alright...and so will I.

With the decision mentally made, my mood starts to lighten now that I have a plan of attack. Pulling around the campus to do another sweep over her street, I noticed a new sign posted in front of a house about five houses down from hers. *Well now, it seems the universe is agreeing.*

Jotting down the number on the sign, I hightail it out of there and head back to mi Mamá's casa for some planning. It takes about thirty minutes to get back on my side of town. Pulling into my mother's driveway, I jump out and head towards the front door.

"Aye, why are you in such a hurry? What's happening?"

"Nothing Mamá, la bendición." Giving my mother a kiss on the cheek, I start to look for the person I need. "Papá, are you here?"

"Oi, back here!" I find my father sitting in his lazy boy in the living room watching telenovelas.

"Papá, can you come help me get some of my stuff from the apartment. I think I found a new place."

"Si, si Hijo. Let me get on my shoes."

Once my father is ready, we both hop into his old truck he keeps in the back and head towards my old apartment. He turns the radio on and Despacito comes up, lightening up the mood. My dad loves that shit, always trying to be 'with it'. I cut him off when he starts singing though, a man can only take so much.

"So what happened Fabian? You don't like the city no more?"

"I was barely there anyways, I'm always hanging out with you guys. Plus, an apartment is like tossing your money away. I think I'm going to buy a house."

"Yeah? You find one already?"

"Yeah, it's near a nice neighborhood. I think you guys will like it." Plus, I'll be near Sakinah. If all works out, but he doesn't need to know that. My father never asks questions about my relationship affairs anyway.

We made it in good time and with my dad's help, we were able to get my stuff in one load. It's kind of sad when you think about it. I barely had anything in there - shit, I didn't even have a couch, just a bed, and table really. A couple of chairs. Damn, this move was a long time coming. I needed to get out of this depressing place.

My dad was able to rearrange some stuff in the garage to store some of the big stuff. Once we come inside, the smell of food floats in the air and my dad plants his ass right back on the lazy boy.

My fingers are dialing the number I jotted down earlier for the real estate agent. I need to hop on this shit before someone else gets there before I do. I *need* this house. Now.

"Hello, you've reached Ace Reality, how may I help you today?"

"I saw the sign in front of one of the houses behind the university. It just got put up today."

"Ah yes, we did just post one today. Did you want to make an appointment to go look at it?"

"Nah, I already decided I want it. What's the price?"

"Sir, are you sure? We highly recommend one of our agents go with you to check the property out, in case you have any questions or concerns?" This shit is giving me a headache. Can't I just buy it and call it a day? Damn.

"Alright fine, who do you have that will meet me there in thirty minutes?" The sound of shuffling papers and movement comes across the speaker before some sounds of typing.

"Okay, we have agent Ken Scotts. He will meet you there in thirty mi-" Ending the call, I grab my keys and start driving back over to Sakinah's neighborhood. It's a good thing it's far enough away from her where she won't hear the roar of the Chevelle. I'm going to have to remedy that issue too. Can't have her knowing I'm moving in.

I make it there in record time and I'm already walking around the outside of the house. Looks solid enough, any work that needs to be done on the inside, I can do. I'm almost hoping it's a piece of shit inside so I can get a better deal on it.

A nice and shiny sedan pulls up the front and an African American male comes out the driver's side door. He's dressed to impress so it's probably this Ken Scotts guy.

"Ken Scotts?"

"Yeah, that's me. I take it you're the one interested in the house?"

"Yup, let's get this show over with because I already know I'm buying it."

"Well, let me get this door lock for you and we can step inside." All these stupid formalities are killing me. I didn't miss the fact that this Ken Scotts character was looking me up and down with doubt when I said I was going to buy the place.

The house tour was taking too long so instead of waiting for him to shut his trap, I started doing a walk-through. Could use some work here and there, some water stains that are barely noticeable but nothing that can't be handled by hand.

"Alright, I saw the place. So what's the asking price?"

"Oh, uh..." He must have really doubted me because he's finally starting to scramble to take out his paperwork on the place. "$310,000 is the current asking price."

"Knock off twenty Gs and I'll buy it in cash." I should laugh at the way his eyes start to bulge but I'm in a fucking hurry here. All those years working my ass off and just coming back to my mother's house for food has allowed me to pile up shit in savings. What better way to spend it than to invest in property and find a way to keep me close to the woman I'm trying to catch.

"I'm going to need to talk to my supervisor but we'll see what we can do." This guy is sweating like a pig, I know for a damn fact I just offered him a good deal. How often does a real estate agent come across someone offering cash?

Crossing my arms and tapping my shoe on the hardwood floor, I nod my head. Agent man starts to dial whoever he needs to dial and after some mumbles and whispers, he turns back around and gives me the okay for the deal. *Good.*

We both head back to the ACE realty office and fill out all the necessary tons of paperwork for house purchases. Damn, they probably felled an entire tree just for this contract alone. When the final sheet is signed, I'm already standing up and stretching from how long I've had my ass planted in their stupid chair.

"Alright, what's next?"

"Well, we'll need the payment for the property." Checking my phone, the bank is still open. I get my ass in gear and take the Chevelle to the closest one that happens to be a few miles away. I hate standing in these stupid places, you swear everyone's got all day to get shit done.

Once my turn comes up, I tell them what I need and I'm handed a cashier's check made out for the house. This stupid trip and last-minute decision is making me burn gas. Pulling back up to the real estate office, I slap the check onto the table and tell them to finish the damn transaction.

"Congratulations Mister Hernandez, you are now the proud owner of-"

"Yeah, okay. Got it. Make sure to send me a digital copy of this paperwork shit too, yeah?" Heading out the front double doors my mind is already trying to figure out another mode of transportation so Sakinah doesn't get suspicious of her new neighbor down the street.

Chapter Seven

SAKINAH

How did this happen? Amir went from asking to telling in the blink of an eye. Was it because Fabian was here? I'm so damn depressed, I don't know what to do.

Have I offended him? I mean, the way he says it makes me sound like a real jerk. Is he right? About the fact that I couldn't even recognize him in front of Amir, that I couldn't admit he's more than just 'a guy'. But if I said anything else, my mother would have started asking questions and I'm just not ready for that. Not with the way she was blasting my life of doomed singlehood out loud in the living room.

This is just a big 'ol mess. One I don't know how to get out of.

And I know I should apologize to Fabian, but I'm scared. Scared to see just how mad he is with my fuck up.

Dammit! *Maybe my mother was right. Maybe I am doomed to be alone.*

Walking towards the adjoining restroom to my bedroom, I start to strip off everything like a snake shedding skin. I need to just remove these depressing thoughts from my mind. I made sure to make the water cold to knock some sense into myself.

But I can't shake the way Fabian looked right before he left. I messed up. Would he ever forgive me? My eyes are burning again with how shitty I feel. They say relationships are difficult, well...whoever said it has never met a Malay girl stuck in the middle of the road between someone you have feelings for and cultural obligation.

Scrubbing my hair quickly, I get out of the shower and stare at myself in the mirror. Who is Sakinah? Is she the dutiful daughter of a Malay family? Is she the one that Fabian so easily called beautiful? Is she the one that Amir sees as his perfect match? My mind is conflicted in which direction is the right one?

Fabian's face flashes in my mind. Why must the decision between him and I be taken away from me before I can even think about it thoroughly?

Frustrated, I leave the mirror and start rummaging through my closet for something to wear. Stupid Amir and his demand for this date. I hate being rude and leaving someone hanging so of course, I'm going to go. He probably knows this and that's why he issued it that way. Tossing aside the nicer things, my frustration comes back full force and I find myself gripping some of the fabric to the point of creating wrinkles.

Why is this happening to me?

Shoving my face into a dress, I scream, letting the fabric muffle my cries. It doesn't change the fact that I still have to get dressed for this date but it does make me feel a little bit better to be able to let go of the tension building within me. My head feels hot and my chest hurts in the worst of ways. I fall to my knees and start to sob, truly. I can only do so much to be strong. I miss Fabian. I miss the way he held me while my world was crashing down again.

Why can't we just be together? Why is my life destined to go through this misery of having something I want so bad be taken away from me?

Wiping my eyes with the dress in my hands, I toss it into the laundry hamper and start looking for something to wear in earnest. I need to get this date over with. Then I will no longer have any obligation. I can tell my mother I tried and it didn't work out. I can let Amir know on the date that I'm not feeling it and set him free to pursue someone else.

Alright, now that there's a plan in my mind, my body starts moving in automatic movements. Picking whatever looks casual but not nice, I start to get dressed and tame my hair for my hijab. I've just gone back into the restroom to make sure my hijab looks okay when there's a knock at the door. The clock on my bathroom wall says six forty-five. Amir must really be looking forward to this date.

Now I feel bad that I'm about to let him down when clearly he must have more than some sort of interest in me.

Grabbing my bag, I walk towards the front of my home and open the door for him. Amir is standing there in a very nice buttoned shirt and dress pants. He even has flowers in his hand like a damn Hollywood movie. Trying to summon a smile on my face, I take the offered flowers.

"Thank you, Amir." I can't bring myself to look at his face. Not yet. Not when it only reminds me of how Fabian left. "Let me put these in something and we can go."

Without waiting for me to invite him in, I can hear his footsteps following me as I grab one of my bigger cups from the cabinet and put some tap water into it. Rearranging the flowers slowly, I know I'm just delaying the inevitable - This date is happening no matter what.

Internally sighing, I close my eyes and pray for strength. Turning, I plaster a fake smile on and tip my head towards the door.

"You look beautiful Sakinah." Why doesn't it feel the same?

"Thank you."

Once we're both beyond the threshold to the front door, the roar of something comes closer. I haven't heard anything like it in this neighborhood before and it's a whole lot louder than Fabian's Chevelle.

The sound starts to disappear and Amir leads us towards his BMW sedan. I bet my mother would be falling over and fainting if she knew we were going on an actual date. Judging by his car, Amir's family is well off. He opens the passenger door for me and I slip inside, taking a deep breath as he comes around the driver's side.

The seats are soft, much too soft for someone who is currently building mental walls around her. I need to see this plan through. Get through the date, make pleasantries, then tell him I'm not interested.

"Sakinah."

"Huh?"

"Is there anything you'd like to listen to in particular?" He's already pulling off my street going who knows where. I didn't even think to ask since my mind's been so busy with what I need to do.

"Whatever you want, I'm not picky."

The drive is quiet and awkward. Maybe it's just me. Looking out the side window, we pull up to a fancy restaurant I don't recognize. But I mean, I don't usually eat out, choosing instead to cook at home because it gives me more time to study.

Amir escorts me inside and the ambiance of the place is supposed to be romantic, I suppose. I feel far from romantic right now. I'm nervous about how long this date is going to go. The server comes by and I haven't even picked up my menu yet. When Amir orders for me I feel beyond annoyed and want to stab his eyes out with one of the forks before me.

"So what do you do, Sakinah?" Didn't my mother give him all the information he needed already? You'd think she'd compile a file and hand it off to him the way she's trying to hand me off like cattle.

"I'm going to the university nearby, studying engineering." He takes a sip of water from his stemmed glass and never takes his eyes off me. It's unnerving.

"Yeah? Sounds complicated. What's a girl like you trying to do with an engineering degree anyway?" Did he just say that? Did I just fucking hear him correctly? Is he implying that women should do other things? I can feel my face scrunching in a frown and school my features. Good. This makes the 'I don't want to ever see your face here again' easier when the time comes.

"Oh, I don't know. Guess I was just trying to make my mother angry because an engineering degree takes longer than she would like. You know, since my eggs are drying up and all."

He chokes on his water and laughs. *Go ahead, choke some more buddy.* The server chooses that exact moment to bring our meals. What the hell is this? My eyes glance at his plate and he has the same thing.

Are these...snails?

"What the hell is this?"

"Escargot."

"Why would I want to eat snails when I have plenty in the garden?" I'm seriously starting to question this guy's sanity, despite not having a garden but there's plenty of these suckers on my flowers and grass back there.

"Sakinah! Don't be like that. It's a delicacy and really expensive. Just try it."

"No."

"Sakinah, let's try to do this. Come on." The fuck?

"What the hell are we trying to do?"

"We're trying to do this dating thing! Sakinah, I've been trying to get your attention since the wedding and you've had your head up in the clouds."

"What the hell is that supposed to mean?"

"What I mean is that I've seen that guy hang around you, and I had to make sure you knew I was in the running. Your mother approves of me, does she approve of him?"

"Him who?" I know I'm playing dumb and I'm fishing. But the audacity of this fucker, acting like he has anything over me, is making my blood boil.

"You know who I'm talking about Sakinah. Are you sure you wanna go out with him? He's not Malay you know." I'm seeing red. My head feels hot, and this fork in my hand is starting to hurt my palm from how hard I'm gripping it.

"We're not going out." I'm practically vibrating as I grit my teeth and tell him this. How dare he?

"Oh, okay, good. Because I remember him saying that he's your brother-in-law, right? Yeah. I guess I have nothing to worry about since he's practically family." Why does the universe feel the need to rub this fact into my face every waking second? I can't stand Amir right now, but I also can't get up and leave since he's my ride here, wherever here is.

There's some muttering going on around us, making me shift my attention from the asshole in front of me to the front of the restaurant. Someone is standing there with a motorcycle helmet on and the server is trying to say something to him.

"Sakinah. Here, let me help you with that and show you how to get the meat out."

"I'm not eating this." Placing the fork down, I cross my arms. This is ridiculous. I lost my appetite earlier with how upset I was but now that I can eat, I can't because all I have is this shit in front of me. Even if I did eat it, it would only be like five bites. Who gets full on five damn bites?

"Come on, don't be like that." I watch as Amir gets up and comes over to my side like he has the right to. My eyes dart left and right, feeling embarrassed right now. Who does this? I'm twenty fucking five and he's coming over to show me how to eat?

"Amir. I'm. Not. Eating. *That.*" He chuckles like I'm being funny when I'm really being dead serious. I'm appalled when he actually shucks the thing out of it's swirly shell and starts to bring it towards me.

"Amir, no!" I'm getting scared, I don't want that thing near me. My hands are up like a barricade and I'm starting to scoot my chair back making enough noise for the people around us to start looking.

"It's okay, it's okay. She's just being dramatic." Amir is telling everyone looking that *I'm* being dramatic? He's the one trying to feed me like a child!

Then he has to go a step further and try to lean in for whatever he has planned but I'm already leaning so far away that I'm almost falling off the chair. What is going on?

He chuckles. I'm starting to get tired of the damn sound. "Sakinah, your mom said I can marry you. She knows I'm pursuing you, so you might as well just go with it. You said so yourself, you're twenty-five now huh. I might as well take the thing I want since it's right in front of me."

What? No! I didn't agree to anything! His lips are already coming towards me and I'm seeing everything in slow motion as I try to push off his advances. He's stronger than I am so I push harder and shut my eyes when I do fall forward and off my chair from his weight disappearing.

Scrambling to my feet, I lift my head to find the biker grabbing Amir by the front of his shirt. Oh, thank god. That was so close, my gut was churning. I thought I was going to puke in his face if his lips touched mine.

"I believe the lady said no." *That voice.*

He shoves Amir into his seat across from me, toppling him over backward making the next table jump up in surprise.

"Sir, sir! You can't do that. I'm going to have to ask you to leave."

"Don't want to eat any of your shit anyway." Fabian turns around and grabs my hand, hauling me out towards the front door. What is going on here? I'm still in shock with how this crazy snail date was going, that I didn't even feel it was Fabian who came in earlier.

When we exit the doors, the fresh air outside makes me able to breathe again. *My god, that was so close.* What is wrong with him? What is wrong with my mother? What kind of guy is she trying to set me up with? Why did I even agree?!

"Sakinah, are you okay?" My eyes do tear up then because...because I thought he was still mad at me.

"Fabian-" I don't know what comes over me but I jump into his arms and cry. Why am I always crying around him? Fabian holds me and the warmth of his leather jacket is soft enough to let us hug tightly. "I thought - I thou-"

"Shhh. You don't have to think anymore. Come on, let me take you home." Nodding my head against his chest, I give him one last squeeze for my own sense of comfort.

We walk side by side down the street a few blocks and turn the corner to find a blacked-out Harley parked in the restaurant's parking lot. How is he going to take me home on *that*? Looking down at my outfit, I'm not sure if this will work. I mean, I'm in cotton pants with a long sleeve top but -

Fabian grabs me and turns me around, putting his leather jacket on me...and his helmet. "But what are you going to wear?"

His smirk brightens up my sour mood as he starts to buckle the helmet under my chin. "I'll be alright, but thanks for worrying. You can make it up to me later." He winks and my heart flutters. Watching Fabian swing his leg over his motorcycle makes me feel things between my legs. How can such a simple act look so damn sexy?

Turning his head, he flicks it to indicate I should get on. *Oh hell.* "Come on Sakinah, just get your ass on so we can go." He turns forward and starts the bike with a roar, the steady vibration can be seen on his handlebars.

Sucking up my fears, the thought of snails and Amir make me place my hand on Fabian's shoulder as I swing my legs over his backseat.

"Hold on tight, okay?"

"Okay." I've never been on the back of a bike before so the momentum from him pulling out of the parking space makes me feel like I'm about to fall off the back. Leaning in, I squeeze his waist tightly as we roar down the street, away from the restaurant - Issac Newton's third law and all that in the back of my mind.

It seems like it took a shorter amount of time to get home than it did to go there. The vibrations of the motorcycle have been doing a number to my lady parts, I've probably wet through my cotton pants from how much it was stimulating me. They never tell you that in the movies. It also doesn't help that every time Fabian shifts or moves, my hands can feel his muscles flex beneath his shirt as the wind whips at us on the ride here.

Fabian pulls up into my driveway right behind my car before kicking the stand down and shutting off his bike. He taps my thigh with his hand and I think he wants me to get off first. Stepping on the peg, I straighten my legs and swing one over. If it wasn't for his other hand holding my thigh and my hand on his shoulder, I probably would have fallen onto the pavement. Fabian swings himself off with ease like he's done it every day of his life even though I don't remember ever seeing him on a bike.

He chuckles as I look up at him through his full-face helmet, his hands delicately unbuckling it for me and pulling it off. It's a good thing I had this hijab on or else, I would have some serious wind-blown hair to tame later.

He smirks again as we both start walking towards my front door. Nothing needs to be said as we both come inside once I get it open. The feeling of relief is immediate and my mind is telling me I should be worried about what he's going to say to my mother. Our families probably run in the same circles after all.

Taking off the leather jacket, I drape it over the arm of the couch as I drop myself down unceremoniously onto the cushions and sigh. How do I get myself into these messes? The sound of metal and something hard taps my kitchen counter and suddenly the couch depresses near me, making me tumble towards his side.

"Well hello there." A cocky smirk is plastered on his face.

Suppressing a smirk of my own, I straighten myself beside him.

"Thank you, for saving me."

"I was going to kick his ass after the date was done anyway." I do laugh then. He can't be serious. "You keep laughing, I'm still thinking about it..once I find out where he lives, that is."

"Fabian! Don't you dare. It was - ugh, it was a disaster waiting to happen. I knew it but I didn't want to stand him up."

"Instead he let you fall down trying to get away from his advances."

"I-"

"Don't. I told you what would happen if someone even so much as tries to kiss my girl. Fucker got lucky he didn't make it all the way. When I heard you crying 'no', I was about to gut him right there in the restaurant and make him the next dinner special."

I should be appalled but my insides are glowing and my cheeks are feeling hot. Turning away from him, I take off my hijab and cap now that I'm home. *What if Amir comes by again? What do I do?*

Fabian pulls me over his lap and I let him. His eyes track over my face and my hair, the longer I look at him the longer I realize that he's not mad anymore from our previous fight. *I'm glad.* It lifts one of the weights off my shoulders. Leaning into him, I rest my head on his chest and wind my arms around his neck.

If I had to be saved, I'm glad it was him. It must be my tumultuous mind that made me do it because I suddenly find myself lifting my head, pulling his towards mine, and pressing my lips against his.

It's the first kiss I've ever given and it's *liberating.*

Chapter Eight

FABIAN

I must have won the damn lottery or something because things like this just don't happen. Not with Sakinah. It's the first time she's ever initiated anything with me and I don't know how to take it.

I used to be the kind of man that just jumps in head first, fuck the consequences because there will always be other women out there. But this girl has wrapped me around her finger so damn tight I'm about to bust a nut just from her pressing her lips against me.

Grabbing her waist, I pick her up and make her straddle me as we continue to explore each other with our lips. She's soft, tentative but growing in confidence the more I let her lead. It's heady to watch her slowly unravel and bloom like a damn flower in the sun.

The smell of her surrounds me, making me drunk off the moment more than any drink would ever do, as she starts to press her breasts against my chest. My hands thread into her hair and the strands feel like fucking silk between my fingers. The moan that accompanies the pelvic grind takes me by surprise and my eyes shoot open to make sure I'm not imagining things. Sakinah's eyes are hooded as she stares right back at me, grinding down again.

Who is this woman? Shit, better to not ask any questions because I'm loving everything she's giving me. Her broken voice floats back into my head and I pull her lips off mine. What if she regrets this?

"Sakinah-" She pounces right back at me and I lose my train of thought. My tongue starts to demand entrance and she opens up to me in invitation making me groan in response. This version of Sakinah is going to bury me, I just know it.

Our position changes and I find myself on top of her as she's sandwiched between me and the couch. *This is a bad idea.*

"Fabian, I want you so bad..." What the hell? She can't say that kind of shit to me right now when I'm trying to be good.

"Sakinah, we don't have to-" My lips travel along her jaw and down to her delicate collarbones. *Fuck, she is so soft.*

"Dammit Fabian, we shouldn't but I want you so damn bad it hurts." My god, what those words do to a man.

"I'm dying here Sakinah. Tell me what you want." Her hand pushes me off her before she seductively takes off her long-sleeve top and holy hell I've never seen such an expanse of perfect skin before. Well, I take that back - the last time I caught her with her nipples poking through her tank top was the last time I saw this much perfection.

Unable to help myself, my tongue dips into her belly button as I create a trail up towards her bra. Fuck, I don't want her to regret this but my dick is starting to hurt.

"Dammit, Sakinah."

"Shut up Fabian and kiss me." *Shit, yes, ma'am.*

Biting the top of her breast along the way, I kiss her with all I have. The room starts to become hot and heavy with the sexual tension between us and all we've done is kiss. Our breathing starts to pick up and every time she moans into my mouth, my hips thrust forward against her covered pussy. I'm torn between ripping her pants off and trying to respect what happened before when she broke down in front of me.

Dammit, what am I supposed to do? My dick is telling me I need to bury myself inside of the woman that's been driving me towards the brink of madness, but my mind is still trying to be a good guy here.

There has to be a middle ground.

"Sakinah, tell me what you want me to do. I don't want you to regret this. I fucking want you so bad but -" She kisses me again but this time much more slowly than the erotic rate we've been going. She stops and cradles my face, her eyes look so sad it breaks my damn heart.

"I don't know Fabian. I don't know." The male in me tells me to fix the fucking problem, but my mind is telling me there is no right solution here.

"Is it really that bad? For two people who feel the way we do...to be together?" Shit, she's starting to tear up and I'm about to slap myself upside the head for making it happen.

"Fabian, I don't know! We can't but-"

"But what Sakinah? Tell me." She's holding something back, I can feel it and it only solidifies my resolve.

Removing myself from her, I stand up and bend down to pick her up in my arms. She comes willingly, wrapping her arms around my shoulder as I take her to bed...

...to let her sleep the night off. She needs to clear her damn head before we make this crap more of a shitshow than what it already is, if what she told me before was correct.

"Fabian-"

"Shh. It's been a long day, you had a lot happen. I'm going to stay here tonight in case you need me." Watching her roll over and cover her face in embarrassment does something to my chest, but I need to be the bigger person here - not the one to drag her into something she shouldn't be involved with.

Forcing myself to turn around, I walk out of her room and lay myself on her couch, staring at her ceiling. My dick is crying for me to take care of it, but right now my mind is cycling through all the possibilities of how we can make this work, without Sakinah getting in deep shit. Because let's be real, I don't give a fuck what it says about me. But Sakinah? I don't want to scar her with my selfish decisions.

Sitting back up, I start to untie my boots and take off my jeans and shirt. Might as well get comfortable if I'm staying the night. My house is down the street but fuck if I'm leaving her alone after that prick tried to kiss her. Just thinking about him makes me want to punch his face in. Good thing I had enough restraint at the restaurant. Vero always told me I had a volatile temper when it gets ignited.

Lying back down on the couch, my hands go behind my head as I listen to Sakinah shuffle around her room getting ready for bed. My thoughts drift back to the way the swell of her breasts rose and fell when things were getting hot and heavy on this very couch I'm laying on.

The sound of the shower comes on and I tell myself, fuck it. I need to get rid of this hard-on so I can at least attempt to sleep tonight.

Bringing one of my hands down under the waistband of my boxers, I grip my shaft firmly, making me hiss. Stroking it up and down, I can feel my stomach muscles tightening with how hard my cock already is. The way Sakinah feels under me, the way her body was writhing...hell, the way she moaned against me all start to play through my head on repeat, like a fucking porno flick.

With each stroke, I'm gripping harder and harder but the climax feels so damn far. Growling in frustration, I take my hands out of my boxers, get up and start to pace her living room.

"Alright, think Fabian." She tells me we can't do this. She tells me it's forbidden. She fucking kisses me like she's drowning yet...

What the hell am I supposed to do? Do I walk away from this? What happens when we have a family get together? What if this spark between us never dies down? What then? Fuck, what if her mother makes her marry some asshole and I have to watch the way he touches her and kisses her.

I'd fucking kill him.

Amir's face comes into my mind and the rage I felt earlier at the restaurant comes back in full force. Slamming my hands on the back of the couch, I hang my head trying to think of something - anything - that will make this shit work. *It has to work.* There's no way around it - I can't stand the thought of my girl with *anyone else* but me.

I stop pacing her floor and start for her bedroom door. I don't know when the shower ended but I'm barging in like a man on a mission - because I am. This is it for me. I can't see myself with anyone but this fucking woman right here. Just the thought of her with someone else makes me want to choke and go on a killing spree.

"Fabian?"

She's in her fucking tank top and shorts again and my mind fills with unbridled lust. Grabbing her, I lift her off her feet and kiss her with all the conflicting emotions running through me. She doesn't disappoint as she wraps her legs around me and starts to give it back just as passionately. Walking us towards her bed, I drop her back onto it as my hands go under her tank top and caress the side of her breast.

Moaning against my mouth, Sakinah's hands pull down her tank top straps, exposing both breasts without taking her lips off mine. *Hot damn.* My mouth leaves hers as they take one of her nipples into my mouth while my hand squeezes her other reverently. *So damn soft.* Her body is writhing under me, her hot pussy pushing against my erection behind my boxers and I almost fucking pass out from more blood rushing between my legs.

Popping my mouth off her, I lift her higher into the bed so her head reaches the other end. Ripping off her shorts and panties, I toss it aside as my hands grip her inner thighs to open them up for me. She's glistening like the damn sun shines out of her pussy and it calls to me. Dipping my head down, my tongue licks upwards between her swollen lips, finally tasting the forbidden fruit that's been causing us nothing but heartache the longer we push each other away. *Fuck, this is turning me on.* I moan against her pussy as I continue to lick up the wetness that's already accumulating.

When my tongue touches her clit, my mouth covers it and sucks. Sakinah gets louder in her cries, her body responding to everything deliciously. *Look at how respon-*

sive she is. Damn, the thought of me being the first down here makes me start devouring her like a starving man. Because honestly, I am. This moment has been long coming. My hands go under her ass, forcing her closer to my face the more she tries to squirm away. Her moans drive me more and more into a zone that makes me want to lose my everloving mind. When her legs squeeze my head, I know she's close. Dipping my tongue inside of her, I bring my thumb up to circle her clit and pinch it on and off. A few more thrusts of my tongue and ...

"Oh my god!" The feeling of her pussy pulsating on my mouth makes my pride and ego swell. Continue to lick her through her orgasm, my hands pull off my boxers, letting my dick breathe from its confinement. With one last lick and suck on her clit, my tongue trails up her body towards her other breast and stops for a small detour. Her intake of air and moans tells me she likes what I'm doing, so I keep going, torturing myself in the process.

But little Sakinah has other plans as she grabs my head and brings it up to hers, tasting herself on my lips. Rubbing my dick against her wet pussy, we continue to duel with our tongues, our kisses becoming sloppy and hot.

"Fabian," she whispers my name between kisses and I can barely make a coherent sentence to answer her. My hips continue to thrust against her, the head of my cock hitting her clit on every pass. Sakinah starts to respond to what my body is doing as she begins to grind up against me as well.

My mind takes that very moment to finally come with a damn solution to our little sexual tension problem. I'm just going to have to do everything I can to not penetrate her. With this decision, I start to grind down even harder until the tell-tale signs of my balls tightening tell me I'm close.

"You feel so damn good against me."

"I'm so wet."

"I know, you're about to get wetter because I'm going to fucking cum." And I do - and it's fucking glorious. Growling against her mouth, my hips start to twitch every so often with how intense the orgasm is. She's coated in me and it makes me want to beat my chest, instead I opt for running my nose along her cheek and biting her earlobe before sucking it into my mouth.

"Oh my god."

"Yeah, Dios Mio is right."

My hips are still slowly thrusting against her as she continues to thrust back. This shit shouldn't feel this good. If I just move my dick a little bit, maybe I can just put the tip in-

"We shouldn't have done that." There she goes again. I groan into the crook of her neck and bite her to punish her for killing my afterglow.

"We didn't do anything Sakinah."

"What do you mean?"

"Don't worry your pretty little head so much."

"What if my parents find out?"

"How the hell are they going to find out what happened in your bedroom?"

"I don't know Fabian! I've never done this before!"

"I know you haven't. I'm glad I'm the bastard that gets to introduce you to it." She slaps my chest and I chuckle.

"Be serious Fabian!"

"Fuck Sakinah! I am being serious. Fuck if I'm going to let any other assho-"

"I mean about what just happened!"

"Nothing happened. I didn't even put it in you. Don't worry so much. Though now that I've had a taste of that pussy of yours, I don't think I can ever go back to not having it."

"Fabian!"

"What?"

"I can't stand you sometimes."

"Yeah? Well, the feeling's mutual. But you have to admit, you feel better don't you?" She giggles. She fucking giggles. Giving her another kiss to shut up her yammering, she melds into me and winds her arms around me tightly.

"For a girl who keeps telling me we shouldn't, you sure are a tease." Nipping her lip, I get up and go to the bathroom to get a washrag. Wiping myself off, I rinse the rag and come back to wipe off the evidence of my...passion on her stomach. *I should make her sleep like that.*

The daggers she's shooting at me with her eyes tell me to hurry up and clean it up. *Bossy little Malaysian princess.* Once the task is done, I chuck the rag into her dirty hamper and climb back into bed with her.

"We should get dressed."

"I'm done with your 'shoulds' and 'shouldn'ts'. Just go to sleep Sakinah."

"Fabi-"

"Shhh.." Pulling her back closer to my front, I nuzzle the back of her head and let out a sigh.

Chapter Nine

SAKINAH

I don't know what to do. We went from kissing in laws to in laws that mess around in bed. *This is bad.* Yet as I lay here listening to Fabian snore behind me with his arms preventing me from leaving the bed...I can't help but feel like a dam has been opened.

Tapping his hand to wake him up, all he does is grumble into my hair. *It's too damn cute.*

"Fabian, let me up."

"Why?" The way his voice is all gravelly makes me scissor my legs. His arm squeezes me tighter as he starts thrusting behind me.

"Fabian!" He thrusts even more and I can feel just how hard his cock is. I'm getting freaked out because what if he's too sleepy to realize what he's doing? *You didn't seem to mind last night.* Shut up brain! "I need to pee."

"Yeah? I can get into that."

"Oh my god, Fabian! Let me up!" He chuckles as he rolls over, releasing me from his restraint. The asshole. Making sure I slap him with the back of my hand at least once, I roll to get out only to have Fabian pull me back and roll on top of me.

My heart starts picking up in speed as he looks down on me. What is he planning? I follow where his eyes are tracking and he's looking at my -

I squeal as Fabian starts sucking on my neck really hard. It hurts but feels good at the same time when he starts to lick at it and suck it again. Pushing at him with all my might, I try to knee him in his dick but he quickly jerks away, laughing again.

Growling at his antics, I get up from the bed quickly and run to the restroom, slamming the door shut. Staring at the mirror, I can see a huge mark where he was sucking. Ugh! The asshole did it on purpose!

A knock comes at the restroom door, startling me. "I know you're looking at it. Every guy close enough to you will be able to see it too."

"You-you-!"

"Sweet and charming lover who doesn't want any stray guy to sniff around his girl? Yeah, that's me. Get your ass dressed so we can go get some breakfast, I'm starving." *This guy.*

Taking a quick shower, I peek out the restroom door to find the bedroom empty. Quickly throwing something on, I try my best to hide the giant hickey with whatever minuscule makeup I have. It's no use, it's just right there! Giving up, I grab one of my little short sleeve shirts and a pair of shorts.

Walking out of my bedroom I see Fabian standing there in just jeans, his naked back making my mouth water. The tattoos on his right upper arm and shoulder spread over part of his back, some sort of black and grey artwork that only adds to his bad boy look. I know I remember seeing some sort of circular tattoo on his left pec but in the heat of the moment last night, I didn't pay it any more attention.

"Mamá, don't expect me over today. I'm going to grab breakfast somewhere else." He usually eats at home? How sweet.

"No Mamá, I know you're the best at making comida. Don't be like that. I don't want you cooking for me all the time." Suppressing a smile, I walk towards the kitchen and start taking out some pans to get started on food. Fabian must spend a lot of money eating out if his appetite is anything to go by.

Opening the fridge, I start to catalog what I have before deciding on what to make when a warm arm go around my waist. Fabian gives me a kiss on the cheek before turning around to continue with his phone call.

"Mamá, there's nothing going on. No te preocupes. I'm not going to starve, geez. Just relax today or something.

I'll talk to you later. Adios." He's so cute. But I'm not going to say anything.

Grabbing some vegetables and eggs, I close the fridge and start on a big omelette. Looking over Fabian's broad back again, I go back into the fridge and look for some beef too. He looks like he needs the protein.

My chopping board is already sitting on the counter as I lean over to my block and grab one of my favorite knives. My mind zones out as my hands start chopping up all my vegetables and setting them aside. Grabbing a plate from the cabinet, I make sure to use another knife and chopping board to cut the meat.

Once everything is set, I start to preheat the pan, standing here patiently with the spatula already in my hand. The eggs sizzle the moment they hit the pan and my hands start to toss in the other ingredients. The heat of the pan is starting to get to me but eggs usually cook quickly.

Sliding the omelette onto a dish I already laid out, I toss in the meat, letting it sizzle and crackle.

"Dios Mio, what are you making in there? My mouth is watering, fuck." Laughing, I turn to glare at him.

"Sit your ass down and wait until I'm done. Don't worry, you'll get fed."

"Why do you have to be like that Sakinah?" Ignoring him, my spatula moves the meat around until there's a brown crisp all over, the aroma filling the house.

"Like what? Like the woman who's making your damn breakfast?"

"You're killing me with that mouth of yours because I don't want to interrupt your cooking and you know it. Feed me woman!"

Sliding the beef on top of the omelette, I grab a fork before heading over to the table where Fabian is seated. Setting it down in front of him, I watch as his eyes go wide with desire. Is this what he looks like when he looks at me? Like I'm something to eat?

"This looks fucking amazing Sakinah. If you didn't already have my heart, I'd rip it out for you right here." Oh...

He grabs me by the waist and pulls me onto his lap, my arms winding around his shoulders. Kissing my neck, I pull away, remembering the hickey from this morning. We don't need any more evidence of what happened between us.

"Oh no, you don't. One hickey is enough." He leans in again and plants a soft kiss on my shoulder.

"It's never enough. I need to let everyone know to leave you alone."

"You're so crazy. Eat your damn food." Growling against me, Fabian chuckles. It's a sound I'm starting to anticipate between us. I love it.

"Yes ma'am. Buen provecho." Fabian practically moans when he places the first forkful into his mouth and I internally preen with delight despite my face not showing it. I've never seen anyone react like *that* before. My goodness.

Getting up, I go make myself a plate of something quick - I guess it will be cereal for today. Fabian's already done with half of this food by the time I come back to sit down next to him.

A few more bites and the plate is practically clean. Where does he put all that? He sits patiently and waits for me to finish my breakfast before grabbing the bowl and the plate to take to the sink. Be still my heart, the man is washing dishes in my damn house. His keen eyes also grab the knives and chopping board.

"What time do you have your first class today?"

"In about an hour."

"Ok good, I'll be back and then I'll take you to school."

"You are?"

"Yeah, why wouldn't I? It's just right there."

"But I usually drive myself."

"The bike uses less gas."

"I can drive myself."

"Yeah, that's cool. But I'm taking you to class."

"Fabian." I watch as he places the clean dishes in the drying rack, wiping his hands on his jeans, and then walking towards me. *He can't take me to school on that thing!*

His damp hands grab my face and gives me a kiss before he says, "Sakinah, I'm taking you to school so everyone can see you're fucking taken."

"But, we're not supposed to-" Another peck on the lips and he leaves me to grab his shirt and walks out the door with his helmet. "What about your jac-" The slamming of the front door makes me want to throw something at the back of his head. The stubborn ass.

Walking into my bedroom, I change into some jeans and a button down shirt that comes to my forearms. I'm going to have to fix my hijab again once I get off the bike. Grabbing my books to make sure I have the ones I need, I hear the roar of an engine coming closer and closer. Fabian barges into the front door. Did I not lock it? What if it was someone else coming in? Jumping and running to the bedroom door, I let out a sigh when I see that it *is* Fabian.

"Fabian! Lock the door next time!"

"Relájate, I'll lock it now. I was only going a couple blocks anyway. Are you ready?" Turning to grab my backpack, I come back out and nod my head.

"Good. You can use my helmet, I'll get you your own after your classes are done so you can get fitted correctly." Why does it feel like he's giving me a promise ring or something? This is getting serious - my own helmet? What if he doesn't let me ride anymore? What the hell am I going to do with a helmet?

"Quit looking like that. You're always going to be in the backseat." *How does he do that?* Grabbing my hand, he hauls us out the front door and ...locks it. *Wait a minute.*

"How did yo-"

"I just made a key for myself. Here's yours back." He opens my palm and drops the key. What the? When did he?

He smirks and leans in to give me a kiss before pulling us down the front steps and up to his bike. *This guy.* I'm going to have to tell him to cut back on public affection. Someone might see us, someone who might know my mom.

Once my helmet is on and we're settled on the seats, Fabian brings up the kick stand up and starts the rumble. The vibration can be felt up my spine, I'm not sure I'll ever get used to this.

We make it to the front of the campus in about ten minutes and my legs are still feeling the vibrations even when he turns off the bike. Getting off, I stand there and wait for Fabian to come help me take my helmet off. His fingers deftly move under my chin as he smirks at me.

"What are you smirking about?"

"How cute you look in my helmet." Slapping him on the chest I give him a glare even though I love this between us - the way we're always fighting like we mean it when we really don't.

Once the helmet is off, I try my best to fix my hijab. When Fabian's hand comes up to try and help, I dodge it subtly making him frown.

"Please, we need to cut back on the touching when we're out. Someone might know my family and news might get back to home." His frown doesn't disappear but his hand falls to his side. I feel a pang in my chest at the rejected look that flashed across his eyes but it can't be helped. We shouldn't have done what we did and touching too much in public will just make us look even more guilty.

When my hijab feels like it's back in place, I turn to look at Fabian to see him putting the helmet on his own head. "When does your last class end?"

"I have to meet Jason for the -"

"What time?" His eyes sharpens with the mention of my partner's name and I start to get worried about what will happen this time.

"I'll call you after I'm done."

"No you won't, you little liar. What time are you guys meeting?"

"Fabian, I need to do this project."

"I'm not stopping you."

"But you're making it hard!"

"How so? I recall being helpful last time."

"There's not going to be a next time, that's for sure. I need to get this project done quickly so then I wouldn't have to meet up with him anymore." Fabian narrows his eyes at me and I narrow mine right back.

"Give me your phone."

"Why?"

"Can you just be agreeable for once and hand me your damn phone Sakinah." With my eyes still narrowed in suspicion, I watch as he takes my phone, shoves it back at me to unlock it, then taps something over and over again. What the hell is he-

"There."

"What did you just do?"

"Don't worry about it. I'll pick you up after class."

"Wha-"

The bike starts with a roar and Fabian pulls out onto the road without another comment. Rude much?

Walking towards my classes, I notice all the girls looking after Fabian's bike. My insides feel a little irrationally angry even though I know it's not his fault he's got that bad boy look down pat - especially with this Harley.

I wish my culture would let me show more public affection, then I'd be able to claim him in front of all these girls. But again, I'm stuck between a rock and a hard place.

Each of my classes come and go and I find myself anticipating seeing Fabian again.

"Sakinah!"

"What?"

"Come on, let's go to the library. I've been looking over all your notes for the project and I think I have an idea of what we can do." How long has Jason been trying to get my attention? Shit, I need to get my head into the game before I fail this class.

Jason is rambling on about something physics related but all my mind can think about is the way Fabian's cock felt against my pussy lips. He didn't even try to slip it in when my pussy was all for it. How can he be that strong? I thought men were all slaves to their baser instincts. Fabian has proven time and time again tha-

"So what do you think? Good idea right?" Jason is whispering since we're almost halfway to the back tables in the library. When we *do* make it to the end, my eyes light up when I see the sexiest man already sitting at our old table, waiting for us. My heart starts to pound and I can feel my face smiling before I even tell it to.

Fabian looks so attractive sitting there with his chair turned backward, smirking at me. How can I feel so strongly for this man before me? I shouldn't. We're family...

"Jason, what's up? Sakinah. Good to see you again."

"Fabian."

"Hey what's up, man? Thanks for the notes, it really got me ahead of this shit. I got a really good idea-"

Funny enough, it becomes entertaining to see Jason start gushing over Fabian's example of velocity. We get a lot done through Jason's ramblings and I'm actually sitting back just watching him blossom into the science nerd he is.

Fabian's input every now and again is actually pretty impressive. It makes me see him in a different light. Beneath the bad boy exterior who seems like he doesn't give a shit about anything is a man with a very sexy brain. When Jason would go on his tirades about things, Fabian would pass little winks at me, and touch my thigh under the table away from anyone's prying eyes.

This game of chance we're playing makes me blush and scared at the same time. What if we get caught? But the idea that we're so close to getting caught is making my blood run hot for him.

When his hand almost brushes between my legs, I shoot daggers at him and he just smiles towards Jason, nodding his head like he's talking about the most interesting thing in the world. How does he keep so cool and calm when I'm turning into a slow-growing inferno for him?

"Alright, sounds good. What do you think, Sakinah?"

"Huh? Yeah, it sounds good." *What the hell are we talking about?*

"We'll see you next week man. Get that model going and I'll see if it jives with the notes we got going."

"Sounds good man, thanks for bouncing ideas with me. Shit, it must be so cool to be sitting on those skyscrapers, putting that shit together."

"Yeah, it's an experience. Ain't nothing like the breeze flowing through when you're sitting hundreds of feet up in the air. Living life on the edge, you know what I'm saying?"

"Damn, you got bigger balls than I do. That's for sure." Fabian is suppressing a grin that makes me want to slap him. I know exactly how he feels about Jason.

"Yeah, you can say that. Sakinah, are you ready to go?" Go? Go where?

"Yeah." Nodding my head and smiling, I just play along so Jason can leave us alone.

"We'll see you next week bro." Fabian grabs his helmet and starts ushering me out the front of the library before I can even say goodbye to my physics partner. The sleek black motorcycle comes into view and my lady parts are tingling. What's going to happen now? Is he going to take me back home and then....then *what?*

Are we going to mess around again? Oh my god. Is he going to ..put it in me? If it feels like I'm falling off a cliff with him just rubbing against me, what would it feel like with him actually inside of me?

My breaths are already starting to come out in small pants when his gaze swings to mine, watching my chest rise and fall. He feels it too because his eyes become hooded when he looks at me. There's electricity crackling between us but we haven't spoken a word. When his hands place the helmet over my head, my breath hitches whenever our skin touches. My eyes are glued to his as he starts to buckle the helmet under my chin. I can feel myself biting my bottom lip in anticipation of what's going to happen - if anything is going to happen at all.

Taking a deep breath in, Fabian smells male - masculine - with a hint of exhaust fumes from his motorcycle. His strong hands flex and I stare at all the veins and tendons working with him as he takes off his leather motorcycle jacket and swings it over me, tucking my arms into the sleeves. There's a smoldering spark starting inside of me as we both stand out here in front of each other. Each touch, each graze is making me burn up, the phantom feelings of his touch lingering long after it's done.

How can these simple movements - that's far from anything sexual - feel so sexy that I'm melting in a metaphorical puddle of goo? I can see his chest rising and falling more than usual as well. When he lets me go to swing his leg over his bike I almost groan with the movement. He has such a nice ass in those jeans of his.

Fabian starts the bike and sticks his right hand out to me. Taking it, I step on the back foot peg and swing myself over the back of him. My arms slither around his abs, sneaking a little touch under his shirt as he pulls away from the front of the campus. Girls milling about are stopping to watch *my man* take me home. It's the only time I really have an excuse to touch him the way I am - I mean, I wouldn't want to fall off the bike, right?

Chapter Ten

SAKINAH

He parks his bike behind my car and we both get off. It already feels so comfortable and right...like we're both coming home. What would it be like to have him with me every day like this? I need to stop entertaining the idea because it's never going to happen - my family wouldn't allow it.

Once we make it through the front doors, all thoughts of family and potential marital obligations go through the window as we both start stripping off our extra layers. Fabian helps me with the helmet and places it gently onto the kitchen counter, but the moment he takes off his t-shirt is the moment my pussy starts to pulse with need.

Oh my god, he shouldn't look this good. He's a danger to all women, especially to me. Fuck, the thought of other women seeing what's beneath his shirt makes me mad.

Taking off my hijab and the layer underneath, I strip out of my shirt as well, leaving me in just a bralette.

Fabian's eyes are burning as his hands start to untie his bootlaces and unbuckle his jeans. My own hands are struggling to take my jeans off since they're starting to shake, making me have to look down and make sure I don't trip and embarrass myself.

When my eyes come back up, they widen in surprise because - because - Fabian was commando under his jeans this entire damn time and his dick is huge and pointing right at me. My heart starts to race from fear and anticipation. Can I really do this? How the hell can that thing fit inside of me?

Casting my eyes up to his quickly, I'm about to do a chicken move and run but Fabian grabs me from behind after only a few steps.

"Easy, Sakinah. Why are you always running from me?" His warm breath coming from behind me calms my nerves only a little bit.

"That thing between your legs is scary as hell, Fabian." He laughs as he lifts my feet off the floor and starts walking towards the bedroom.

"Yeah? Maybe it just wants to get to know you?"

"It already got to know me."

"Maybe it misses you."

"I don't know about that."

"Sakinah, Sakinah, Sakinah. Why are you always like this?"

"Like what?" I squeal as he tosses me onto the bed, landing me in a cloud of comforters and pillows.

"Like a little brat that wants it but just can't admit it."

"I don't know what the hell you're talk-" He climbs over me like a panther on the hunt and I'm caught by surprise - though I shouldn't be - as he covers his mouth with mine. It's always been the way he subdues me. Maybe he's right. Maybe I *am* always running, but I can't help it. The unknown is too scary.

But when his hands caress my face, and his soft lips coax mine...he always makes it a little less scary resulting in my surrender.

The feel of his warm skin under my hands, the way his muscles flex as he brings us closer together - it's all just so much stimulation for me. My mind isn't sure what it wants to concentrate on. When our tongues start to tangle and dance, I'm lost in a sea of overflowing emotions and thoughts that I didn't realize he was trying to remove my panties. After a few moments, there's the sound of a snap and a sting on my skin making my eyes shoot open.

"Fabian!"

"You can buy more." Did he..did he just rip my damn panties off? I can't keep buyi-

His lips are suckling on my neck again and the pain and pleasure he's eliciting from me is making my toes curl. When I feel his teeth graze across my skin, my heart picks up speed but Fabian knows just how to make me relax again when the flat of his tongue starts to go over my pulse.

"Are you hot for me Sakinah?" How the hell do I answer that? I'm nervous again - he's so much more experienced than I am.

"Maybe." He chuckles and starts to move lower and lower - I can't keep my eyes off him, curious about what he's going to do to me. His hands come up and pull down the cup of my bralette and my eyes widen when he literally tugs at my nipple ... with his damn teeth. He pulls it back into his mouth and the feeling of his tongue swirling around it makes me want to squeeze my legs shut but I can't because his large body is blocking me.

The light kisses he plants down my torso makes the butterflies in my stomach start fluttering in utter chaos until he dips his tongue into my navel and bites the skin right beside it. My body starts to squirm and my head falls back the moment I feel his lips start to suck again, knowing he's going to leave another mark on me. At least it will be where no one can see it.

I don't know what comes over me but my hand starts to push him lower, where I really want him to be. It felt so good to have his mouth on my pussy that I crave it again but I'm too embarrassed to ask.

I guess I don't have to since Fabian starts to chuckle against the inside of my thighs as his fingers glide between my folds that's already so wet down there. The sensation is so teasing it makes my stomach muscles tighten in anticipation.

"Fabian, please…"

"Please what?" His fingers rub up and down some more. It's too much and it's too little.

Biting my bottom lip, my pride doesn't want to admit that I want his mouth on me. Can't he just..just feel my need?

"You want me to lick your pussy, Sakinah?" I gasp at his crude language during the moment. Why does it make me so hot?

"You want me to eat you like a damn buffet? Because I'm a hungry man and I do like to eat." His tongue teases my folds but it doesn't go where I want it to go. Would I be too greedy to ask for more?

"Are you going to feed me Sakinah? I love a woman that can feed my appetite." I'm turned on and pissed off at the same time. I should be the only woman who feeds Fabian's appetites. Grabbing his head, I pull him right up to where I need him because he does this shit on purpose to piss me off.

"Yes, Fabian. I'm going to feed you right now..I need you to eat my pussy." He groans right into me as his mouth covers my pussy. The feeling of his tongue dipping inside of me makes my hips thrust forward, wanting him deeper.

Fabian Hernandez has made me a greedy woman. My hands thread through his hair as my body starts to react to every single little thing he does down there. Why does this feel so damn good? When his warm mouth covers my clit and his tongue starts to flick the hood, my body bows off the bed, my legs spreading wider for his assault. I feel so wanton...but at the same time I feel so free - free to just feel and enjoy this moment between us behind closed doors.

All the teasing today and the bike has made my lady parts sensitive, it seems, because I can already feel myself climbing, the sensation wanting me to chase the finish that feels so far but so close.

"That feels so good." He groans again into my pussy and the vibrations almost tip me over the edge. I'm just about to fall off that cliff, my legs squeezing him between me, my stomach muscles tightening when..

He pulls his mouth off me and starts to climb my body. I'm so mad!

"Fabian!" His chuckle and smile soothes my soul as he starts to kiss me, making me taste myself on his lips. I greedily do so as my tongue starts to lick across his top then bottom lip before dipping inside to entwine in his.

Wrapping my arms around him to bring him closer to me, I don't feel his hand creeping down my body. Not until a hard slap jolts me.

His mouth starts to increase in passion, preventing me from getting a damn word out as he slaps my pussy again.

This asshole! Some of his slaps are hard, some are soft and each time the palm of his hand rubs against my clit to soothe the sting I feel myself loving every moment of it. He slaps hard a few more times and I cry out between our lips - that is until his fingers start to stroke my clit with vigor, sliding down my wetness and back.

Fabian tilts his head and bites my neck again just as his fingers hit that perfect spot and suddenly my body is twitching and writhing in ecstasy as my fingernails grip onto his shoulders for dear life. The harder I grip him the more he growls into the crook of my neck, telling me how much he likes me being rough.

Naughty Fabian isn't done with me yet though as he brings his hand up and sticks his wet fingers in my mouth. His eyes blaze as he watches me suck them, his hips thrusting against me. Is he going to put it in me this time? This is so bad - I shouldn't want it so much. The feeling of his hot and hard cock rubbing against me makes my legs open wider in invitation. I know I shouldn't but...

Fabian pulls his wet fingers out of my mouth, trailing it along my cheek before covering my neck with his hand. I should be scared, he could easily choke me if he wanted to, I'm at his mercy and drunk on everything he's doing to me. But my heart tells me that I know the real Fabian, not the bad boy everyone thinks he is - but the man that holds me when I need it most, the man that continues to come back no matter how much of a brat I become out of my fears. This is the man I'm staring at right now.

Our eyes lock on each other as his hand gently squeezes, making my legs wrap around his body in response. His hand pushes up against my chin, forces my head to tilt back as he starts to suck and nip my shoulder all the way to my collarbone. His dick continues to slide against me but never in me and I start to become frustrated with need as my pussy starts to grip onto nothingness - wanting him inside of me so badly.

On a particular thrust, I swear I can feel the tip of this cock almost going inside of my core but he pulls his hips back, making me want to cry.

"Fabian, I need you so bad."

"I know baby, but we can't." Dammit! Is this how he feels when I tell him we can't? Because it's already killing me! "Goddamn you're so fucking wet for me."

"I need you inside of me."

"Shit, don't tempt me."

"Fabian, please!"

It seems like every other stroke, the tip of his head butts up against my opening and when I try to wrap my legs around his tighter to bring him inside of me, Fabian pulls out like the tease he is. This push and pull continue on for what feels like an eternity of torture when all of the sudden his hips falter and he cums onto my lower abdomen. I want to scream at him but I also want to kiss him because he's so much stronger than I am.

I've noticed that even when Fabian climaxes, he still continues to thrust. When the tip of his cock hits my clit, I hold my breath wondering if he's going to put it in me now that his hot pulses are starting to die down.

But much to my frustration, he doesn't. Instead, he just chuckles, covering my mouth with his, removing his hand from my neck to grab onto his cock and rub the head of it all over my clit just to tease me even more. This asshole.

"You're so dirty Sakinah. We're supposed to be good."

"What the hell about what we just did qualifies as being good."

"You're still a virgin. Don't worry so much."

"Shut up Fabian! I'm not worried, I'm just so fucking horny and want you inside of me!"

"Dammit Sakinah, don't do this to me. I'm trying really hard here."

"I love it when you're hard."

"Dios Mio."

"Fabian..."

"Sakinah, stop. You know we can't. You've said so yourself." Pulling his forehead against mine, I close my eyes in frustration once more because he's fucking right. We shouldn't even be letting it go this far, yet...it feels so right to be this way with the person you l-

"Fabian." My eyes start to tear up again at the messed up position we find ourselves in. It shouldn't have to be this hard, this complicated. Two people should be allowed to feel deeply for each other and just...be.

"I know." He kisses my eyelids before wiping away my tears with his thumb and getting up to go to the bathroom to clean up.

Sweet Fabian always comes back to take care of me, cleaning me, wiping away anything that might make my mind break down to tears. When he climbs back into bed to hold me - he doesn't realize that he's already broken me in the best of ways.

Chapter Eleven

FABIAN

Sakinah and I have developed a new pattern to our ...so called non-relationship. We wake up together, I take her to school, then go back to move my shit into the house down the street. Sometimes when I'm done early or just want to take a break, I bust out my phone and watch it track all her movements as she walks all over campus.

She probably doesn't realize I'm doing it, but what she doesn't know won't hurt her. I mean, it's good to know where your loved ones are, right? In case she needs me, I'll know the exact location she needs me to be. That's another good thing about getting this bike, I can weave in and out of traffic faster to get to her.

I think Jason and I have established an understanding. He knows she's off-limits, so I don't worry too much about it. It doesn't mean I'll let him sit next to her alone though. I'm not stupid.

After returning my dad's truck from the last load, I take the bike and bring it around the student parking lot of the university. Was it really just the other day that Sakinah was running away from me, making me chase her ass here just to get a kiss from her? How times have changed.

I regret nothing. It was all worth it to get to where we are now.

Turning off my bike, I swing my legs off and grab my phone out of my jacket. There she is, sitting in class. The dot hasn't moved for a while but I know her class is about to end. Taking off my helmet and hanging it on the handlebar, I walk towards her last class of the day - Statistics.

I've studied the layout of this campus and have found every nook and cranny near every single class she has. Why? Well..

"See you later Sakinah!"

"Sakinah! There's a party that's coming up tonight to celebrate the end of the semester. You should join us!"

"I'll think about it." Her head is still turned towards the sea of students spreading out as they start walking towards all the different classes they have. Grabbing Sakinah, she gasps as I pull her into a dark corner and into one of the unlocked closets nearby. She doesn't scream because we play this game daily. Me finding her and hiding her so we can stave each other off until we can finally be together at home.

The closet is dark enough with a privacy glass that no one would be able to see us even if they walked by, but light enough for us to see each other as we both start to kiss each other desperately, aware that time is of the essence until one of us gets caught. Sakinah has become bolder and bolder as time goes on, expertly kissing me back and making me want to fall to my knees and worship her right here. But she always has to wear so many damn layers, frustrating the hell out of me, teasing me to no end. My hands grab her ass as she moans into my mouth, tempting me to just say fuck it and take off her pants right here, right now.

But like every time we do this, she pushes me away with a sultry look, fixing her hijab and blanking her face right before she leaves me and joins into the sea of students walking about in the hallways.

Slamming my head against the wall, I give myself a little time for my dick to die down. What am I doing right now? What is my thirty-something-year-old ass doing sneaking around with a student? If the shit between our families doesn't make this forbidden, hiding our sexual misdeeds in closets surely does. But fuck if it doesn't drive me to want her even more.

Once my breathing calms down, I open the door slightly ajar to make sure there aren't too many witnesses as I walk out casually like nothing ever happened. Of course, my leather jacket stands out in a building full of nerds but I can't do anything about that. The breeze that greets me once I make it outside makes me take in a few lungs full of air as I walk towards my bike to wait for Sakinah.

The sound of feminine giggles following my wake starts to annoy me because I know damn well Sakinah doesn't do that. My head is about to burst with how much I just want to stick my dick in her and just claim her as mine for everyone to see - but I can't. I should. But then she'd kill me. If not her, then her family would kill her - then she'd be pissed at me. And I don't want Sakinah pissed at me - I love it more when she loves me. At least I think she does, if the way her body responds to me is anything to go by.

What if she's only using me to explore her sexuality? The thought pisses me off to no end but I tell myself that I'll just have to try harder to make her want to stay. Leaning against my bike, I find my mind brooding again over the possibility of Sakinah and I being together. How can we make it work?

Do I just take her to Vegas and marry her ass so she can't go anywhere? Would she even want to? Fuck, I've never had to plan this far before with anyone I've ever been with. To be honest, I've never felt this much before for anyone I've ever been with. She's different. She's under my skin and I feel like it's hard to breathe when I'm not around her. I need her scent around me all the time which is why I had to keep calling my mother to tell her I'll be eating elsewhere...and also why I haven't slept a day in the new house I bought.

"Hey." My eyes snap up like an automatic response to the voice that's continued to haunt my days and nights despite hearing it in person just as much. I can already feel my face muscles stretching into a smile when I see her standing before me in the sun, looking as stunning as the first day I saw her.

"Hey, are you ready to go home?" Her smile lights up my fucking life everytime I see it. Is this what love is like? Looking forward to the little things like a damn smile, like you need it to keep you living. I've never felt like this before, so I wouldn't know.

The ride home makes my heart feel full and tight. *Home.* We've kind of made it that way, haven't we? I already have a couple of pairs of clothes at her place to change into. I don't think she noticed me slipping it in, if she has she hasn't said anything about it.

Parking the bike behind her car, I swear I see a BMW drive by. It's noticeable in this neighborhood full of students who can't afford anything that shiny with their student budgets.

Walking into the front door, Sakinah drops off her back-pack and veers towards the kitchen to start on food. This woman is amazing, just watching how she flutters around the kitchen so expertly makes my dick come back to life. I've had to stop wearing boxers because too many layers were becoming restricting with the constant hard on I have around her. Jeans over my dick aren't any better but I need some sort of protection when riding the bike to and from her school.

"What are you making me today?"

"Who said I'm making you anything?"

"Sakinah."

"I'm making myself a plate of something. You're welcome to make your own."

"Aww don't be like that. I love your cooking!"

"Yeah? Well, what if I decide not to cook? Are you going to starve to death?"

Growling, I get up from the chair and start walking towards her. Her eyes get wide but I can still feel the brattiness coming off her as she stares at me like a kitten with her claws out. Caging her against the kitchen counter, we stare at each other some more. This stubborn woman...

"Are you going to let me starve Sakinah? Is this how you feel about me?"

"Food has nothing to do with how I feel about you Fabian."

"Yeah? So how *do* you feel about me?" I'm fishing, but can you blame me? My mind has been in circles about this non-relationship we have going. I don't know where I stand with her and I've admitted to myself that it kind of scares me a bit. I don't like feeling this way.

Her hand cradles my face, but her eyes tell me she's going to spew something that makes me pissed.

"Well..."

"Well what?"

"For one, you're a pain in my ass."

"Yeah? The feeling's mutual."

"You're lucky you're hot and I keep you around for decoration."

"That's cold Sakinah." She giggles at my face as she pulls me down for a kiss. This girl right here drives me nuts. She pulls away from me but keeps her lips just a breath away.

"Fabian, the way I feel about you...it's too much. It over-whelms me and sometimes scares me. I don't know and yet I feel that deep down inside I do. But I'm scared, Fabian. What are we doing?" We stand here in silence for a few moments as I let her words soak into me. I'm scared too but my mind is telling me to just fuck it and take her. Take all this shit as it is, fuck everyone else. How can something so damn perfect - so damn right - be wrong?

Sakinah places a gentle kiss against my lips once more before she winds her arms around me in a warm embrace and we just hold each other, trying to comfort each other in this shit we're in. We're not going to be able to hide this much longer, not with my growing feelings for her. I can't always be a dirty little secret she keeps behind closed doors.

But today is not the day to decide on it just yet. No, today we can just be Sakinah and Fabian in the kitchen, about to eat a nice meal together while the world goes on outside without us - without bursting our bubble we have going on in here.

Sakina breaks the embrace and shoves me out of the kitchen. "Go sit down Fabian, I'll make you something to eat." At the mention of food, my stomach growls and she laughs. It's the lightest sound but also raw. I haven't heard her laugh like this until a few weeks ago when we've finally started to let our true personalities free, getting to know each other.

Whatever Sakinah is making is causing the house to smell damn good. When she places the plate piled high with whatever it is, I impatiently wait for her to sit down with her own plate so we can say Bismillah.

"Buen provecho." I start to dig in and almost cum right there. How can this little woman cook like this? Does she not taste her own damn cooking?

"I got invited to a party with some of my classmates." I'm barely hearing it as I continue to shove mouthfuls of this amazing meal into me.

"I think it will be fun. I've never been invited before. I should make an appearance right?"

My plate is almost finished when she kicks me under the table, almost making me drop a spoonful. What the hell?

Wiping my mouth with the napkin she has on the table, I glare at her. "What the hell was that for? I was trying to enjoy my meal."

"I was trying to talk to you about something! Listen!"

"Alright, alright. I'm listening. Tell me again." She lets out an exasperated sigh and it's the cutest thing.

"I said I'm going to a party tonight. I got invited today. It'll be fun. I need to go out and mingle and all that. It's college, this is what college people should do right?"

Flashes of my own years of partying play before my mind - images of girls all over guys and guys all over girls, drinks overflowing cups and a whole lot more I don't wish to remember. I don't think I like the idea of sweet little Sakinah around that kind of shit.

"No."

"No, what?"

"I don't want you to go."

"Why?"

"Because they'll be guys there. They'll be all over you trying to get into your panties. No, I don't like it. No."

"Who the hell made you my dad anyway? You can't tell me I can't go."

"I just did."

"Fabian! I'm going. I want to go. I finally got invited to something. I don't want to be an outcast."

"Who said you're going to be an outcast? Parties happen all the time. I'll take you to some."

"No! It's not the same as you dragging me somewhere. *I* got invited, I'm going."

"Why are you like this Sakinah?"

"Like what? Why are *you* like this?"

"I'm like this because I know damn well guys only go to these kinds of parties to fuck all the drunk girls."

"Is that what *you* do at all these parties?"

"Yes! That's why I know you shouldn't go." Her eyes sharpen and I think I just stuck my foot in my mouth. She looks pissed and there's practically steam coming out of her ears. Trying to rewind our conversation in my mind, I'm barely even able to comprehend what just happened when she starts to yell.

"Get out!"

"Wait, what?"

"I said. Get. The. Fuck. Out!"

"Sakinah, let's talk about this. I wasn't trying to make you ma-"

"Fabian! Get the fuck out of my house!"

Shit.

Chapter Twelve

SAKINAH

That asshole! He tells me he goes to parties to fuck girls yet I can't go to the one party I'm finally invited to? The thought of him fucking other girls when he hasn't even stuck it in me makes me want to scream. In fact, I walk to my bedroom, pull out his clothes he's been hiding in my damn dresser and scream into it to muffle the sound.

He drives me insane! I'm so damn mad I want to cry but I'm too pissed to cry. Nothing fucking makes sense and it makes me angrier.

Oh, I'm going to this damn party especially since he doesn't want me to. Stripping out of my clothes, I turn the shower on cold to try and cool my temper. Fabian always does this to me, either he drives me up the wall or drives me crazy with lust. I can't control myself around him.

Scrubbing my hair a little extra hard, I rinse myself and everything off and get out still pissed at what just happened.

"This asshole thinks he can tell me what to do." I mumble to myself as I start drying myself aggressively with the towel in my hand, wringing out my hair.

"Tells me he can take me parties like he's fucking still going every damn week or something." Tossing the towel towards the hamper so hard, I miss it but leave it there anyway.

"Says guys only go to parties to fuck drunk girls. I don't even drink!" Grabbing a more form fitting outfit off my hanger aggressively, the hanger flies off and falls to the floor making me even more pissed since I have to pick it up.

"I'm going to show him and his stupid pretty face that I can handle myself just fine at a party. I'm twenty fucking something years old. Where does he get off telling me what to do?" Bringing the dress I'm gripping to death towards the restroom, I hang it on the doorknob while I start to lotion my body up with something that smells nice. Forgetting to grab a bra and panties, I take the dress off the doorknob and toss it onto the bed.

When I put the dress on, I try to smooth out the wrinkles I made. It's form fitting - more than usual - the neckline a little lower than my others but my hijab should cover it. The fabric drapes nicely, showing off my curves without showing off too much skin. The fact that the sleeves only go to my elbows makes me feel risque already. Good. I need this. I need this party to lift my mood.

Letting my hair dry before wrapping my head, I look in the mirror one more time. Being around Fabian has made me more confident in myself. Every time he touches me and tells me how beautiful I am and how smart I am. I can already hear my mother's voice in my mind yelling at me about what I'm wearing. But I need this. I need these small little victories for myself, to break free from the restraint I keep feeling.

Grabbing my bag with my necessary items, I head out the door and make sure to lock it securely. When I turn around I swear the back end of the car that just drove by looks familiar. Shaking my head, I think about the party and start walking towards my car. I haven't driven in a while and it almost feels weird. Fabian's been taking me to and back from school practically every day since this thing between us started.

Ugh! Why can't I stop thinking about that asshole? *Okay, party. I'm going to a party. Let's do this.*

Pulling out my phone, I input the GPS to the location where I was told the party was being held. My eyes glance at the clock on the dash - the party's been going on for about an hour now. That's alright, I shouldn't come in that early anyway. It looks like the house is not too far from the campus, kind of like mine but on the opposite side.

Pulling out of my driveway, I turn on the radio to drown out any more thoughts of Fabian. The trip only took about fifteen minutes and the street is already starting to fill up with parked cars. Finding a spot a few blocks off, I pull the car next to the curb and put it in park. Using the car's mirror to check my hijab again, I let out a breath and gather my courage to enter this party like I know what I'm doing.

My dress flows with the breeze as I walk towards the music that's starting to blast through the front door of the house party. This really is just like the American movies I watch, my goodness. Friendly faces hanging outside wave at me, some with plastic cups in their hands.

Entering the house, the air is thick and warm from all the bodies everywhere milling about in different groups. Some are on the couch hanging out, some are standing to the side. My eyes dart around trying to find a familiar face as I continue to walk deeper and deeper into the house.

"Sakinah!" Turning towards the voice, I see Jason shoving people aside to get to me. He looks different, looser, calmer. My eyes shoot to his cup and assume he's already been drinking. I'm going to have to be careful.

Fabian's words echo in my head but I try to not let it get to me. I'm going to enjoy myself at the party.

Some of the other girls from class find me and I hang out with them in their little group. Everyone's excited about the semester ending, getting closer to our goals and our different degrees.

One of the girls hands me a cup and I become leery. "I don't drink."

"Oh don't worry, this is just punch." Sniffing it, it does just smell like some sort of fruit punch. When I taste the first sip, it's cool against my lips and I don't taste anything funny so I keep drinking as the girls and I talk about things from our projects to cute guys they've been trying to hit on.

A few hours later and a few cups later, my head is starting to feel funny. I'm also starting to feel really warm but everything around me is starting to go in slow motion. Am I just tired? Maybe I should leave the party soon before I fall asleep behind the wheel. I want to take this hijab off and feel the air against my head to cool down. It's a good thing this place is only about fifteen minutes away. The girls and I have taken over the couch and when I go to stand up the world starts to spin sideways a little, freaking me out.

What's happening to me? How am I supposed to drive home when the world can't even stay still? Stumbling a little bit, I make my way out of the living room towards..towards somewhere away from the partygoers.

"Sakinah, are you okay?" It's Jason's voice but I don't know which direction it's coming from. Not until his hand touches my arm to steady me. I'm glad he's here, maybe he can tell me where the restroom is so I can pee and then go home.

"J-Jason, do you know where the restroom is?"

"Yeah, come on, I'll help you." We're walking towards the stairway, having to go around so many people hanging out in random places, everywhere. How can this many people fit into one house, I wonder?

"Hey, I'll take it from here. Our families know each other."

"Yeah?" Jason sends me a look but I didn't even catch everything the voice was saying. Something about family. Damn, if my family saw me like this right now I'd be in so much trouble. They sent me to school to get a degree, not to party. It's a good thing I'm already doing well in all my classes.

"Sakinah." When did I start sliding down? Or is it forward?

"Sakinah. Come on, I'll help you." His voice is different. This isn't Jason. When I turn my head, the room spins a little but when it stops, Amir's face is right next to me. What the hell?

"Amir? What are you doing here?"

"Keeping an eye out for you. You shouldn't be here. You're lucky it's me who found you and not someone else. I won't tell your mom, but you can't do this anymore." What is up with these guys who think they can keep acting like my dad?

"I need to pee."

"Alright, let me see if I can find the restroom. I think it's upstairs." Upstairs is right because it feels like I'm tasked to climb a damn mountain with how many steps there are. Why are there so many steps? My bladder is about to explode from the amount of punch I've been drinking.

"Alright, I think this is it. Go in and hurry up so I can take you home." Whatever. I knock on the door first in case there's someone in there. No response. Opening the door I step inside and make sure to lock it - well it took a few tries, but I locked it. The feeling of peeing is almost orgasmic as my bladder finally finds relief.

Getting up, I wash my hands and look at myself in the mirror. I don't look any different. Maybe my eyes? Why do I feel like this? Was there something slipped into my drink? My heart starts to beat harder at the thought and Fabian's words come back to me. Maybe he's right. But, it was the girls who kept bringing me drinks. This doesn't make any sense.

The knock on the door makes me almost jump out of my skin. "Sakinah, are you alright? Hurry up. Do I need to go in there?" Come in here? For what? To help me pee?

"Why the hell do you need to come in here?"

"What are you doing in there?"

"I was peeing, what do you think I was doing? It's what I said. I needed to pee." Unlocking the door, I'm thrown back a little bit as Amir barges inside and then shuts the door behind him. What the hell?

"You have a fucking mouth on you, Sakinah. I don't like that shit. When we get married, you're going to have to learn to respect me as a husband."

"Who said I'm marrying you?"

"Your mother. You think she's going to be happy to hear her daughter is hanging out behind closed doors with her brother-in-law, hmm?"

"What the hell are you talking about?" Why is he so close to me all of a sudden?

"Every time I come by, his motorcycle is there. Every time I come by to see you in class, he's picking you up. I can't get any time with my fucking future wife when there's someone blocking me. Is that why he came to get you at the restaurant? Were you already fucking him by then?" Future wife?

"I'm not your damn wife." The sting on my face starts to bloom into something. I didn't even see him raise his hand but my face is telling me he just damn well did.

"Did you just fucking slap me? You asshole!"

"You need to know your place, Sakinah. I can't have that fucking mouth of yours spew shit like that when we go out as a couple." The audacity of this fucker right here.

Whatever is happening to me right now must make my inhibitions go down because I'm screaming at his face.

"Get the fuck away from me! I'm not your damn wife!" Amir has a look of distaste on his face but the knock on the door stops him from doing whatever he's about to do.

"Sakinah! Are you alright?"

"Jason!" Amir covers my mouth with his hand as he answers.

"We're fine! I'm going to take her home. She's not feeling too good."

"She was fucking fine when I left her." The doorknob jiggles and I'm praying Jason gets in here so he can get Amir away from me.

"I said she was fine!"

"Then why the fuck don't you let her answer?" Jason busts in with his shoulder to the door, slamming it back and Amir lets my mouth go. My mind is still working slowly, trying to figure out what's happening.

I think Jason and Amir are yelling at each other but my hands are grabbing my phone in my purse as my fingers fumble on the screen. Please please please, come on! Fabian must have put his number on my speed dial, because there's his face right there under favorites. Hitting the button, I hear the phone ring just as my eyes shoot back to the guys who are starting to shove each other.

"Sakinah. I'm on my way."

"Fabian, I'm so scared."

"Shit, I'm halfway there. Hold on." My mind is trying to comprehend how he even knows where I am but I'm just glad he's coming. I don't know what Amir is going to do if he takes me home. The boys are still yelling and staring each other down blocking the doorway. I can't get out of this damn restroom.

The music is too loud to know if anyone is hearing us and this fight that's about to break out, but suddenly a hand pulls Jason back and punches Amir in the face, making me scream. Amir gets up and grabs Fabian before he can get to me, but Fabian must have been anticipating it because he turns quickly and grabs Amir by the throat and slams him down in the hallway.

Oh my god. What the hell is happening? Scrambling to get out of this damn restroom prison since the boys have created an opening, I make it to the doorway when I hear Fabian growl.

"Stay the fuck away from my girl. The next time I see you anywhere near her, I'm going to kill you, you feel me?"

Amir is choking out his answer but I'm stunned with his response as I stand behind Fabian.

"You mean my fucking wife? Yeah, her mother has already given me the okay. She's already mine. You're the one that needs to fucking stay away from his sister-in-law." I just about die right there when the tail end of his response echoes into the hallway making those who are left around us staring at the show before them. I can feel my cheeks getting hot, I'm so embarrassed. Of all the ways for our secret relationship to get exposed...a party was not what I envisioned.

Fabian's back tenses as he lifts Amir up by the neck and slams him into the wall. He looks so enraged and I don't know how to stop him. No one else does either because everyone starts to go down the stairs or back away. Jason is standing a few feet away but he's not saying anything. What *can* you say?

Watching Fabian bring his elbow back stuns me as he lands two more fists into Amir's face before letting him drop to the floor. Blood is starting to ooze out his nose but he's not moving. Is he dead?

Fabian turns his face to me and I can see the storm of emotions raging behind his eyes as he comes towards me and lifts me bridal style, making the room spin. Wrapping my arms around him, I bury my face into his chest and close my eyes to stop all the motion from making me want to get sick. He continues to descend the steps as the music continues to blast in the background. No one says anything, not that I can hear anyway. I know we make it outside when the air changes, becoming cooler from the sun having gone down.

The sound of a metal door opening tells me Fabian came over with his Chevelle. He tries to put me into the passenger seat but it's just too much of a change in position, so I latch on even tighter.

"Sakinah, I need to take you home. We have to put your seatbelt on okay?" *I'm scared. What if the world spins again?*

His warm hands rubbing my back make me feel a little bit better. Relaxing some of my tension, I open my eyes slowly to make sure the word still looks the same. Fabian kisses me on the cheek before pulling the seat belt around me and shutting the door. The air that whooshes in from him opening the driver's side feels good on my skin. It is definitely time to go home.

Chapter Thirteen

FABIAN

I knew she shouldn't have gone to that shit. I knew it! But I'm not stupid enough to bring it up right now. No, instead I'm going to stay the night and take care of my girl.

That fucker Amir is lucky I didn't kill him. There were too many people watching us. But when he called her his wife... all my insecurities and fears about my relationship with Sakinah came bubbling out, like a volcanic eruption of emotion.

Carrying her into her house, I place her gently on the couch as I go to the fridge to find some water for her. She needs to sober up. I just bet someone gave her spiked punch because she'd fall for that - she's too innocent for that party scene.

Coming back, I sit her up slowly and keep her right beside me so she doesn't topple over. Twisting the cap off the bottle, I hand it to her.

"Sakinah, you need to drink some water. Come on, it'll make you feel better."

"Okay." Watching her closely, I make sure she doesn't spill it all over the place - and she doesn't. *Good.*

"I'm staying the night. Someone's got to make sure you're okay." She drinks almost half the bottle in one go and hands it back to me. Putting the cap back on, I place it on the little coffee table she has in her living room.

"Okay." Her body slowly starts to fall towards me and I lay us both down on the couch. She's too drunk to even keep a sitting position. My adrenaline is still dying down so we might as we both relax for a minute.

"Thank you for coming."

"Sakinah, I was coming for you anyway."

"I'm glad." Her face nuzzles my chest and my hands wrap around her tighter. That fucker's words still make me want to break something but I can't move right now. When Sakinah's breathing starts to slow down, I carefully straighten her up and carry her into the bedroom. Removing her shoes and hijab - or whatever it's called - was easy, but this dress? Where the hell is the zipper? Does it have a zipper? How the hell did she even get it on?

I feel like I'm flopping her around like a ragdoll by the time I figured out that it's a pullover type outfit. Holy hell, who makes this shit? It's a good thing she's pretty much passed out at this point because she doesn't rouse with all this movement at all. Taking off my own shoes and shirt, I head out to the living room to bring back her bottle of water and another one just in case and place it on her nightstand.

Taking off my jeans, I start to rummage through her dresser only to find my clothes missing. *What the hell?* Looking around the floor I see a bunch of stuff strewn around haphazardly, some of which are my damn clothes. She must have been really pissed at me today. Well, she can stay pissed because I said what I said.

If I had left the house any later -

Shit, I don't even want to think about it. Grabbing my boxers off the floor, I slip it on and get into bed behind her. She's still in her bra and panties so she can't be too mad at me when she finally wakes up.

———

SAKINAH

I'm laying down somewhere. Opening my eyes, it looks like my room. There's water on the nightstand and suddenly my throat is so dry. Grabbing it, I finish off the one that's half full and put the empty bottle back on the nightstand. Closing my eyes, I turn over and am met with a lot of flesh - very masculine smelling flesh. *Fabian.*

He rescued me again. Snuggling into his side my mind starts to drift off but not before Amir's voice starts echoing quietly into my ear.

Something jostles me awake. Fabian starts to move an arm behind his head and my head lands on the mattress. How long was I asleep? I woke up last night, didn't I? I think I drank some water. Blinking a few times, I stare at Fabian's sleeping form. He really is a beautiful specimen of a male. Studying the planes of his abs and biceps, my body starts to respond. He's so hot, and he's always lying next to me practically naked.

Looking down at myself, it seems he's stripped me to my underwear. It's making my resolve melt more and more. This relationship of ours should have never grown into what it is but after Amir blasted the fact out there...what the hell do I have to lose now? Everyone already knows.

Lifting my head, I scoot closer to his side and place my chin on his chest, staring at his jaw. He hasn't shaved in a while and it shows. He's looking even more gruff than usual, the motorcycle doesn't help either. I didn't miss the fact that early on at the party some of the girls nearby were talking about the hottie on the bike that comes by.

My fingers trace each of his abs one at a time. The dip on his hip leads my fingers down towards the boxers he has on. He must have found it on the floor since I remember getting pissed and throwing it down there. That's another thing about Fabian, he's so good at rolling with the punches.

Oh god. The way he punched Amir and stopped him...it shouldn't be hot, but it is. It makes me want to .. oh I don't know.. I'm not good at this relationship stuff.

Running my hand softly down and around his waistband again my mind goes to all the times he's put his mouth on me. It feels so good. I wonder if I can make him feel good too. My heart starts to pound a little harder in my chest. What if I do it wrong? I mean, all you do is suck...right?

My face gets hotter just thinking about putting him into my mouth. I bet Fabian never gets embarrassed about putting his mouth on me. My legs start to scissor as I climb over him even more. Pulling his boxers down that's starting to tent anyway, his dick pops out and almost slaps me in the face. Holy shit he's big. I've never seen a dick this up close before. Shit, he's the only dick I've ever seen...or felt.

His dick is bouncing a little and it's scary. Does it have a mind of its own? How am I supposed to put it in my mouth if it moves like that? Blame it on the residual liquid courage because my hand grasps his shaft and Fabian moves a little bit but still doesn't wake up. His skin is so soft and his dick is so hard at the same time. Moving my hand up and down, I start to build a steady rhythm and feel a little braver. Pulling his dick towards me, my tongue licks the top. That wasn't so bad, but now I'm really damn horny. Just knowing he's still asleep makes me want to swallow him whole. *Maybe I should try.*

Putting my entire mouth on him, I suck him down between my lips until it feels really far inside. Is it? What do girls talk about at school? Deep-throating? What does that mean? Does that mean I shove him all the way down my throat? My god, he's way too big for that.

Pulling my mouth off him, I lick the top and swirl my tongue around the crown of his dick. This shouldn't be so sexy. Sucking him down again, I hear Fabian groan in his sleep. On the next pass up, my tongue tastes something different. *Oh my god.* I'm so hot right now. I need more of this - I love seeing his reaction to me. It makes me feel powerful and sexy.

Rearranging my body over him so I'm straddling his legs, I start to suck him up and down in earnest, learning to relax my jaw to try and take in more of him. There's no way this man will fit down my throat. The farther I take him the more I start to occasionally hit my gag reflex, and every time I do, he moans. My eyes glance towards him now and again but Fabian is still sleeping, the only change being his change in arm position from behind his head to the side of him.

Fabian has some big hands. Thinking about the way he slapped my pussy makes me squirm on top of him. On an upward pass, I feel hands threading through my hair and when I swing my gaze to his, I see that he's looking at me through half-lidded eyes. *He's so fucking hot.*

When my mouth takes him in again, Fabian tilts his head back, thrusting his hip towards me to take him in even deeper. My mouth starts moving faster and his hand starts to grip my hair harder and his hips slowly start to fuck my face.

"Fuck."

I like the way that sounds. I really do want to fuck him because it's getting really hot and really wet between my legs. My panties are soaked and the friction is killing me.

"Get up here." Giving his dick one last suck and lick at the tip, I crawl up his body. He growls when I take too long and pulls me up until his lips crash against mine.

"You're so fucking bad Sakinah."

"I know."

"That's what I fucking love about you." My heart stops at the mention of the L word and suddenly I want it all. *I want all of Fabian.*

"I need you inside of me."

"We can't, remember?"

"I'm so horny."

"Come here."

He grabs two handfuls of my ass and pulls me down onto him to grind. But it's not enough. These damn panties are going to give me a burn between my wet lips.

"My panties."

"Don't worry about it." Fabian's finger roughly pulls the crotch of my panties aside as he starts to slide his dick against me. It only does so much when my panties keep getting in the way.

"Fuck, stop wearing panties to bed." Fabian rips off another pair, snapping the elastic against my hip causing a burn against my hips but I'm too lost in lust to care.

Sitting up straight, my hands go behind me to unhook my bra as Fabian kicks off his boxers. We come back together, flesh against flesh, my nipples rubbing against his chest in the most agonizing way. Fabian has sucked on my nipples so much, they've started to become chapped. But right now they're crying to be sucked on again for some relief.

"Fabian, I want you to suck me." He groans and pulls me up until my nipples are right above his mouth. The head of his cock is right at my entrance with this change of angle and I'm feeling brazen. Moving my hips over him, I can feel his head dipping in and out ever so slightly. What would it feel like if he went all the way in? He's so big, would he even fit?

"Stop grinding on me like that Sakinah, it's going to slip in."

"Then let it."

"Dammit woman."

"I want you Fabian."

"Fuck." His mouth moves to my other breast and I can feel that shit down to my pussy. Shoving my hands between us, I grab his dick and squeeze, making him groan and suck my nipple harder.

Rubbing the head of his very hard cock against my clit, my body starts to move to a sultry dance even I'm unaware of. It's like it knows what it wants and it's trying to convince him to come inside.

"Sakinah." His voice comes out like a plea as he starts to lick the top of my breasts and try to push me down lower. Scooting back, we both slip a little, the head of his dick sliding in and stretching me. *Oh my god.*

"Shit, you're too big."

"Dammit, Sakinah." Fabian's arms go around me and he flips us over and onto my back.

"Fuck, you feel so good."

"I want you so bad."

"Shh, shh. I got you."

Fabian starts a slow and shallow thrust, dipping the head of his cock inside my wet pussy and I want to cry from how good it feels. *I need more!* My legs wind around him, trying to pull him into me and he thrusts in what feels like another inch making me frustrated.

"Shit, you're so fucking tight. Are you sure?" After what happened at the party, I've never been more sure about anything.

"Yes, Fabian! Please!"

When he pulls his hips back slowly, the feeling of his dick leaving me makes me want to whimper in protest until he thrusts back into me, filling me up and stretching me in the most delicious and painful of ways.

"Oh my god. I feel so full."

"Dios Mio Sakinah, I'm not all the way in yet." *Shit.*

Fabian kisses me and distracts me as he continues a slow thrusting motion. I'm so damn wet he's literally gliding in and out of me with little resistance - until he gives me one hard thrust and fills me to the hilt, making my mouth open in a hard gasp.

"Let me take care of you." Once the feeling of being impaled starts to slowly dissipate, my mouth starts to respond to his kisses.

A few thrusts in and the sensations inside of me starts to lean more towards pleasure instead of awkwardness. It helps that Fabian's been rubbing his thumb on my clit during his slow thrusts because now I need more. *Is this hungry feeling ever going to end?*

"More." He chuckles against my lips as his hips start to move faster. "It feels so good."

"Yeah? You like that?"

"Fuck yes."

Fabian grabs the back of one of my legs and throws it over his shoulder before he starts pounding into me, making my breasts bounce and making me feel like I'm about to be pounded right off this bed. *Holy crap.*

"Shit, you feel so fucking good around my dick."

I can barely breathe right now with how hard he's ramming that monster between his legs into me. The sound of wet flesh on flesh fills the room accompanying the smell of sex. It's getting so hot, I feel like I might internally combust any moment. The sensations he's drawing from within me is starting to feel like a chase.

Fabian twists his hips somehow and I almost squeal. *What the hell?* He keeps changing his pace while his hand continues to pinch and roll my clit in the most delicious of ways. When he forces my body sideways and pushes my lifted leg farther back, I feel like a damn acrobat. But whatever he's doing is making me feel so damn close to the finish line that I want to cry.

Watching the way his dick slams into me must be what it feels like to watch porn because I'm getting even more aroused from the sight. The way his shaft glistens each time he pulls out of me only to ram it back in just as hard - The way his abs flex with his hip thrust forward.

I must be going out of my mind because I'm starting to feel even more full, like he's getting bigger. His hip thrusts falter a little bit and I think I feel it throbbing inside of me as I watch him pull his dick out, cumming on my pussy lips and all over my clit. His free hand is gripping the head of his cock and rubbing it hard against me that it pushes me over the edge.

"Oh my god."

"Fuck yes. Cum for me Sakinah." He rubs the head of his dick against me even harder, still pulsing cum all over and between us as I try to suppress my cry of pleasure, my body tumbling over the precipice as I watch Fabian rub his cum everywhere between my legs. How can a man produce so much? It's so erotic it makes my mouth water.

Letting my leg go, Fabian falls forward and kisses me as he continues to slowly thrust his shaft between us. It's not as hard anymore but still feels just as sexy as when we started this whole situation.

The situation being...I just gave my virginity to Fabian Hernandez, *my brother-in-law*. Once our breaths calm down and our heart rates start to slow, Fabian rubs his face against my breasts, making me laugh.

"Stop."

"Why?"

"You're being weird."

"No, I'm not." His lips pull one of my nipples into his mouth again as he starts to suck and nip.

"Fabian! Stop."

"You didn't tell me to stop before."

"Asshole."

"I know." He turns me and slaps me hard on the ass right before he gets up and gives me a smirk. He stands at the edge of the bed with his hand out towards me. "Let's go shower."

His dick is still glistening from everything that's happened and I think I will. In fact, I feel like a fully glazed donut.

"Okay."

Chapter Fourteen

FABIAN

Showering with Sakinah is a new experience. In fact, she's the only girl I've ever showered with because most of the girls in my past left before I could even wake up. This..this is nice.

Well, it would be nicer if it wasn't so fucking small in this stupid shower. Damn, how the hell is a man like me supposed to even scrub himself?

"Quit squirming around."

"I'm not squirming, this shit is too small."

"Well, that's not my fault."

"Are you saying it's mine?"

She splashes the loofah over my chest and starts to scrub again, pressing her body even closer to me as the loofah travels down to my dick. Seems she likes to pay close attention to it as it starts to become semi from her ministrations.

"I think it's pretty clean by now." Lifting an eyebrow I watch as her lips tip up into a sly smile.

"I'm not sure. Maybe I should take a look."

"Why would you need to take a look?" Grabbing her hand, I force it around my dick that's now rock hard with thoughts of her on her knees in here. As nice as it would be, this shower doesn't have enough room for that. I'd be fucking her head against the damn tiles giving her a concussion.

Turning us so the water is hitting my back, I push Sakinah against the tiles in front of me. "Wrap your leg around me." She has her moments when she does what she's told because she likes what I give her.

Grabbing my dick, I start rubbing it against her hot center. Watching as the water droplets run down between her breasts, my eyes go over the curve of her body. She's so damn soft and feminine - it makes me hot knowing I'm the *only* man allowed to touch her like I do.

Leaning my arm against the tile, I slip my dick slowly inside of her, watching it disappear. It's the most erotic sight, the way her chest starts to heave up and down - the way she tries to get away from me only succeeding in pressing herself against the tile even more. Before my dick can make it all the way in, my hips are pulling it out just as slow and Sakinah whimpers. She acts like she doesn't want it but every time I'm about to pull out, she looks like she's going to kick my ass for even trying.

I do love her fire.

Pulling out all the way, I rub my dick against her wet folds again and kiss her so she can't say anything sassy. Thrusting back into her, she gasps into my mouth and my tongue dives in, simulating the motion my dick is working. Her hands have come up to my chest, running her nails down, making me want to thrust my dick harder. It's her little play, but I got her number. She's not winning this.

On a particularly hard scratch, my hips thrust forward until I'm all the way to the hilt, jostling her enough to break our kiss when her head falls back.

"Hold onto me." She does as I lift her ass up to wind her other leg around me, letting me pound into her the way she wants it. I'm going to have to be careful here because Sakinah's pussy feels too damn good. I think I pulled out in time when we were in the bedroom. The memory of her pussy covered in everything I gave her makes my abs and balls start to tighten. I'm close already. Shit. Pulling out of her, I drop her legs down and cum over her mound again, just watching as jets and jets of it keep coming out like it knows she needs to be claimed this way.

Sakinah's mouth is biting the top of my pecs making me hiss and my dick throb even more. She drives me fucking nuts.

When it's all said and done, we wash ourselves one more time under the cold water and finally get out of the smallest shower known to man.

———

It takes Sakinah a few good days before the light bruising on her face disappears. I had to take her to the drugstore to get some makeup. It did a pretty decent job but it doesn't hide the fact that I know how it came to be. It burns me up every time I see it, my mind working different ways I can kill the fucker and not get thrown in prison. Maybe if I get Omar to call his b-

"Fabian, are you listening?"

"No. I'm thinking of ways to kill Amir."

"Fabian!"

"Are you serious right now, Sakinah? That fucker hit you! He needs to be buried six feet under."

"Fabian, you can't."

"Just you watch me -"

"No! What if you get put in prison? Then who am I going to have to protect me huh?" Fucking smart ass sexy woman. She's right. Now I have to think of other ways -

"Fabian! Stop thinking about it!"

"I'm not."

"You're lying! I can see it in your face!"

"What kind of face is that?"

She plants her ass on my lap as I sit at the kitchen table, winding her arms around me and rubbing her little nose against mine.

"It's the same face you made when you came to save me." Tilting my head, my lips brush hers and she melds into me. Our kiss is soft and slow, a constraint on the emotions brought up by the memory of that stupid party. Our tongues start to dance when there's the sound of someone slamming on the window, breaking us apart.

Turning our heads to the side we see...her mother staring at us both, pointing her fingers and yelling something in Malay. *Oh shit.*

There's someone standing behind her - someone male - and my hackles rise because I already fucking know. Amir leans down and smiles his shit-eating grin as Sakinah's mother starts towards the front door, pounding on it.

Sakinah jumps off me and covers her mouth, her eyes wide, not able to say a damn thing because we're caught red handed..by her mother of all people. Fuck!

"Sakinah!! Open the door!"

"Jahanam! Shit! Fabian, what do we do?"

"What can we do? She already saw us. We're just going to have to suck it up and deal."

"She'll kill me!"

"No she won't. It was going to happen sooner or later, you know that."

"But not like this!"

"We can't control everything." More knocking comes through, much more aggressively than before.

"Sakinah! I know you're inside huh! Open the door!"

"Fabian!" She wants me to rescue her but this is the only way. We have to come clean, I'm tired of hiding us anyway. Tired of having to hold back my feelings for her in public when all I want to do is shout that she's mine at the rooftops to every fucking male that looks at her.

Taking one for the team, I go to open the door. Sakinah's mother doesn't even look my way as she barges in right for her daughter. Amir, though, he doesn't dare to step over the threshold because I'm already killing him twenty different ways with my eyes.

Lifting my lips in disgust, I shove the fucker farther out and shut the door in his face. I hear Sakinah in distress and her mother yell, "*Aku sepak!*" I turn to find her mother grabbing onto her arm and kicking her while Sakinah yelps and tries to run away. *What the everloving hell?*

Grabbing her mother by the arm, I pull her off my girl. Mother or not, that shit is just too far. "You need to stop."

"What will everyone think? Auntie Zunai sure will embarrass me for this! Allah, how embarrassing!" She throws her hands in the air before she starts wringing her hand like a damn witch about to cast a fucking spell or something, eyes darting from her daughter to me. I'm so confused.

"You two will bring shame to my family! Sakinah! You need to marry Amir so no one hears about this! You cannot marry your brother in law, no!" The tiny woman is walking around the house looking for something. My face scrunches in confusion as I watch Sakinah's face morph into pure fear.

Her mother comes back with a damn broom of all things - didn't I say she was a witch? - and starts to chase Sakinah who escapes to hide behind me. *What the hell am I supposed to do right now?*

"Ibu! I don't want to marry Amir!" Her mother lunges like a little jackrabbit and starts to pinch Sakinah in the arm, making her cry out, while trying to whack her ass with the broom. Pulling it out of her arm, I keep it over her head so she can't get to it again.

"People will be talking behind our backs! How could you do this? You need to marry Amir!"

"No!" Sakinah is shoving her mother off her as much as she can but her mother latches on like a damn leech on a mission to suck the life out of her.

"Sakinah! You need to not shame the family! You cannot do this to us!"

"Ibu! I love him!" Her mother shoots daggers at me right before she ignores me again and proceeds to kick Sakinah in the shin, hitting mine in the damn process.

My temper starts to rise as I toss the damn witches broom aside, grab Sakinah's mother and lift her up kicking and screaming something I can't understand, taking her towards the front door. My hand struggles to grab the damn doorknob but I get it to open and shove her outside with a still smirking Amir.

Shutting the door on both their faces, the pounding starts up again. Sakinah runs into my arms, crying her heart out as her mother says something that makes my girl shake even more.

I don't know what the hell is going on, but I know it isn't good. How are little Asian women so damn vicious? Flashbacks of my own mother with her wooden spoon and chanclas come to mind and I retract the thought. Mothers are *all* vicious, especially when they're pissed to that degree.

But hell, Sakinah is a twenty-something-year-old woman. She should get more respect than that. No wonder this relationship's been confusing her and making her mentally break down.

Some more yelling and screaming comes from the other side of the door and I can feel Sakinah gasp and grip me tighter around my middle. *What is going on?*

The sound of footsteps getting farther and farther away releases some of the tension I was holding. Rubbing Sakinah's back, I kiss the top of her head and hope she can stop crying enough to tell me what her mother said.

"Fabian."

"What is it? What do you need me to do?"

"Fabian she-" This girl is killing me with the suspense.

When Sakinah lifts her head up to look at me, my heart breaks. What is this look? What the hell did her mother say?

"Fabian, she disowned me because I brought shame to the family. I-I can't go back home and - and she's going to take this house away from me."

Well damn.

"What do I do? Fabian, I'm so scared! Where do I go?"

Holding her tighter, I shush her and rock her. We can work this out. It's not so bad. "Sakinah, it will be okay."

"How can you say that? I don't have anywhere to go. I can't go back home!"

"Sakinah."

"My family, my sisters-"

"Sakinah."

"Fabian, my-" I kiss her on the lips to stop her damn talking. The tactic works because she deflates a little, letting go of some of the anxiety she's holding onto.

Putting my head against hers, I breathe slowly in and out to make her follow suit and she does.

"Baby, you're my girl. Why would you need to go anywhere other than with me? If you say no, I'm taking your ass there anyway because I can't wake up without you."

It gets her to laugh a little as she deflates even more. "Fabian...how did we get to this?"

"To what? Listening to my girl breathe fire and yell at her mother that she fucking loves me?"

"Dammit Fabian, you know what I'm talking about." She's getting shy, hiding her face from me but now that I know the truth, I can take this crap shot in stride.

"I do. We can finally just be together, Sakinah. I can finally kiss you-" pressing my lips to hers, she looks at me adoringly and it makes my heart want to burst. "-in fucking public and tell all those fucking guys around you that you're taken."

She playfully slaps my chest and gives me an honest laugh. *Good.*

"You drive me nuts."

"You do me too, but I can't live without you. Move in with me?" She gives me a soft smile and nods. "Come on, let's get your shit and go."

Chapter Fifteen

SAKINAH

Fabian drove to his mother's house and switched out his bike for his dad's truck, bringing it back to the front of the house. The only big items we took with us were the couch and the nightstand. According to my *boyfriend,* the couch held too much sentimental value to leave behind. My clothes and books didn't take up too much room and we decided to leave the sedan behind since my parents had provided that for me as well.

During my mother's spiel on the other side of the door, she told me that I wasn't allowed to live in the house or be provided for anymore. It was heartbreaking knowing your own mother can so easily say those things to you.

But it is the way of our culture. I *knew* this relationship was going to put me in the hot spot, I just didn't know it would get *this* hot - boiling and scarring my heart. But I wouldn't change my choice for anything. I don't want to marry a potential wife beater - not that my mother even has a clue about that. I bet Amir conveniently never mentioned anything about it, for her to be pushing me his way.

Fabian would always be my first and final choice. We were always meant to be together. No matter how hard we tried to stay away, the universe kept throwing us right back to where we started with the fire between us stoked even higher.

Getting into the passenger side, Fabian walks around and slams the driver's side door shut. His father's truck sounds as much of a tin can as his damn Chevelle; All these old cars are full of metal. Hopefully, no one runs into us, and does it even have airbags?

"Don't give me that look."

"What look?"

"You're offending the old clunker. He runs just fine."

"Clunker indeed..."

"Now, now Sakinah. What are you trying to say? You're hanging out with my rusty ass too. I'm probably classified as vintage."

Laughing my ass off, I shake my head. Fabian is just too much.

"Yeah, well, you're stuck with me now, old man."

"Good. I was going to kidnap you soon anyway." I stare at him in disbelief as he gives me his signature smirk and wink.

Pulling out from the sidewalk, he drives what feels like half a block and pulls to the side to park. I'm sitting here baffled, wondering if we forgot something when he says, "We're here."

How did I not know this asshole lives about five houses down from me. Looking out the window in skepticism, I see his Chevelle sitting in the driveway. *No wonder I haven't been hearing it drive by. He's been keeping it here the whole time.*

"Fabian..."

"Yup! I knew you'd like it. Now get your ass out and help me bring this couch inside."

"Fabian! How long have you been living here?"

"Long enough to fix all the shithole up on the inside, waiting for you to come to this moment." This asshole *boyfriend* of mine always has a way with his words that make you want to strangle him and kiss him senseless at the same time.

No wonder he's been staying at my place, it's no different than staying over here.

After maneuvering the couch through the door and placing it down, I straighten up and look around. It's sparse and very Fabian - always looking like he's gone with the wind wherever the wind takes him because he just doesn't care.

The layout inside the home is actually not that far off from what my old house looks like. Pushing Fabian's handful of clothes aside, I start hanging my dresses in neat and tidy order. Sometimes when my life feels out of control...I find myself starting to control what I can - in this case, the closet.

"Hey, are you hungry? I can eat a damn horse."

"You're always hungry."

"I don't have jack shit in this fridge. What do you feel like eating?"

"Whatever you want. Just don't get any pork for me."

"Got it."

His phone rings right at the very moment and my ears perk up when I hear him answer.

"What do you want? Fuck, stop yelling at me, I can't understand a damn thi-" A knock comes at the door and I drop the dress I'm holding. It can't be my mother right? She doesn't even know I'm staying with Fabian.

"What's up, man." The sound of flesh on flesh hitting each other makes me run out the bedroom to find Akmal shaking his hand and Fabian rubbing his chin while his head is turned to the side.

"Akmal!"

"That's for my sister."

"Alright, alright. I feel you. I wanted to punch you too when my sister brought you home."

"That's the thing Fabian, you never brought her around at all. She's not your fucking dirty little secret."

Fabian lets out a booming laugh and I'm wincing because isn't that exactly what Fabian's been telling me about how he felt the whole time we were hiding our relationship?

"Akmal, it isn't like that." How can this crap blow up so damn much in such a short period of time?

"Are you pregnant?"

"What? No!" Akmal turns his glare back to Fabian and I'm getting offended on his behalf.

"Did you fucking knock her up and get her kicked out of the family? Hasanah called me and told me what happened. What the fuck do you think you're doing with my sister, you asshole?"

"What I'm doing with Sakin- cabrón what the fuck do you think I'm doing with her?" Dammit, Fabian!

"It looks to me like you're taking advantage of *my fucking virgin sister*."

Fabian stops rubbing his chin and starts to lean down towards Akmal, making me scared he's going to knock him out.

"Take advantage? Let me tell you something *brother*. What I'm *doing* with *your* sister is keeping her fucking safe from assholes like Amir who slaps the shit out of her while trying to do what *your mother* wanted and marry her - trapping her in a fucking life of punches and fucking foolery. *What am I fucking doing with your sister?* I fucking *love her* enough to not let her go through that shit!"

My heart stutters. Fabian is fuming, his back tense, his body heaving breaths in and out as his hands fold into fists...but my heart - oh my fucking heart - did not miss the fact that he just yelled out that he loves me.

Akmal's eyes are shooting from Fabian to me and back again. The tension in the room is so damn thick, I'm choking with it. It looks like people outside are starting to slow down when they walk by, trying to see what's happening in this fucking house.

"Then *brother*, I expect you to do the right thing and make this shit *right*."

My brother turns around and storms out. What the hell has my life turned into? A damn soap opera?

Fabian slams the door, locks it and walks to the couch to grab the phone. Was that thing still on this whole time?

"Vero! Your fucking attack dog just came by! Keep your fucking esposo on a damn leash." The sound of Vero's voice yelling from the other end is loud but I can't make out what she's saying. Fabian's eyes lock onto mine as he says, "I fucking love her. Don't worry about it. I know how to take care of what's mine." His hand ends the call and tosses the phone back onto the couch and he continues to stalk towards me. I'm stunned again by how easily he just throws out the L word to anyone who's willing to hear it.

He continues to stalk towards me and I'm captivated by the hunger in his eyes. This is it, isn't it? We've made our stand with our families. We've chosen *us* over obligation and guilt. My eyes are burning again with how momentous this moment really is - from my fight with my mother to Fabian throwing his love for me around for anyone to hear.

We've chosen our path.

We both start stripping where we stand as he continues to stalk towards me like a predator, ready to claim his prize. I'm feeling hot and too constricted anyways, wanting to shed the old me away. Does this mean...does this mean I don't have to wear my hijab anymore? I didn't even remember to put it on after what happened with my mother. I'm down to my bra and panties when Fabian takes off his pants, showing me that he went without boxers, his dick proudly pointing at me, telling me what he wants.

Unhooking and tossing my bra aside, I slide my panties down my legs, bending over the arm of the couch so he can see just how wet I am for him.

Fabian doesn't play this time as he comes up behind me, grabs a fist full of my hair and shoves his dick into me in one go. I feel so full, so overflowing in this position with my legs closed together that when Fabian covers my back and hisses in my ear, I almost combust right there.

He pulls my head back enough to suck and bite on my neck as he pounds my hips into the arm of the couch. He's right, it does hold too much sentimental value to be left behind. My hands are outstretched onto the cushion to prevent me from tipping all the way over. Fabian fucks me like he's trying to make a point and I love every second of every pound that's probably going to leave bruises once we're done.

He's twisting his hips again as he rams it into me and I can feel myself wanting more and more of everything he has to give me.

I can feel the warmth of his chest pressed against my back as he leans over me, removing his hand from my hair and instead holding me across my chest, grinding his dick into me deeper and deeper. The sound of our combined juices squelching loudly in the living room but we both could not care less at this point.

"I love the way your pussy feels, like it wants to swallow me whole. Is your pussy hungry for me Sakinah?"

"Yes." His hips are hitting mine again, harder and without the twist making my breasts swing wildly as I try to hold myself back from toppling over this damn couch. I can feel his arm move as it grips onto one of them, holding me in place as his thrusts start to falter and his dick starts to almost grow bigger inside of me.

When his mouth latches onto the crook of my neck and he growls, I know he's cumming - but this time he doesn't pull out and I can feel the warm jets of his cum shooting inside of me, making me feel so dirty it almost throws me over the edge...almost.

As his thrusts become slower and slower and as his tongue starts licking the wound he probably left behind, Fabian pulls out of me making me cry out with the abrupt change and turns me around. He lifts one of my legs onto the arm of the couch, spreading me wide and open, holding the small of my back preventing me from falling as his fingers start to thrust inside of me like it's another round.

Our kisses become sloppy and hot, passionate and uncaring. His thumb slowly circles my clit as his other two fingers penetrate me and start to curl into a spot I never knew existed. A few more strokes inside like that and I fall over the edge, crying out in ecstasy, trying to hold onto his shoulders for support because my legs have suddenly become weak like jello.

What the hell was that witchcraft? My mind is still in a daze, confused at how fast he made me orgasm.

He kisses my lips and grounds me back into reality, his wet fingers trailing across my hips before his hands grab my ass and pulls me closer to him, pressing our bodies as tightly together as they can go.

"You're fucking mine Sakinah, and I'm going to make sure everyone knows it."

Picking me up, I wrap my legs and arms around him as he walks us both towards *our* bedroom.

Chapter Sixteen

SAKINAH

After the confrontation with my mother and my brother, our days have been relatively peaceful. Fabian brought his bike back home and our usual drop offs and pick ups continued. I don't know what he does while I'm in class but he's always on time no matter how early or how late my last class goes.

It's the most curious thing.

Fabian and Jason have a sort of..little agreement going ever since the incident at the party. Jason has been dubbed Fabian's extra eyes. Well, more like Fabian threatened him about watching my back or else he'll be next, but it's close enough I guess.

The project was done when Fabian decided to bring his Chevelle so he can transport the little building model he has made for us. We were the only group to get an A on it.

With classes ending, it leaves me with one last semester in the university before I don't ever have to return. I'm glad I had a full scholarship since it means I won't have to worry about paying anything back once I'm done - I don't want to add any financial strain to what Fabian and I have going on.

The roar of Fabian's bike in the distance makes me smile and look up as my hair blows into my face. I've slowly started to stop wearing my hijab. It was almost an unconscious decision until Fabian noticed the pattern. I guess my subconscious mind was trying to tell me to shed my old life and the things that used to hold me back.

The smell of exhaust fumes and the heat of the bike as he starts to pull up near the curb is what I notice first. Next is the shiny new helmet strapped to his backseat, the one he recently got for me so he doesn't have to give up his. Lifting his visor up, Fabian turns off the bike as he tries to tell me something.

"I can't understand you." He takes off his helmet and hangs it on his handlebar before pushing his short hair back. Some girls have stopped around us to watch and I take that moment to pull his face towards mine and give him a proper hello kiss. It was beyond liberating the first time I did it and it took Fabian by surprise even though he was the one who brought it up. I love that he continues to respect me no matter what his opinion is on the matter.

With a final chaste kiss on the lips, we pull away and smile at each other.

"I was saying - before you interrupted me - that we should go see my mother. I haven't been over in a while and she's probably worried."

"Oh." This makes me nervous. I've never met anyone's mother like this before. I've never had a boyfriend before. I've only recently had *the* talk with Vero on the phone the other day.

"So you and Fabian huh? What did he do?" She sounds so accusing. I shouldn't be surprised since Fabian is trouble.

"What do you mean?" Best I ask to make sure.

"Did he make you be with him or what? Did he force you? Use his manly charms on you?" Force me? Fabian's not like that.

"No! It wasn't like that. Not at all. It's-It's complicated." How do I even begin to explain our relationship?

I mean, yes? It kind of started that way but our emotions started mirroring each other the more we found ourselves together. It was just me and my own mind warring over something that was meant to happen anyway.

"Girl, I know 'complicated'. Tell me the truth about everything so I don't have to go over there and kick his ass." A laugh bubbles out of me because Vero's personality is just as intense as her brother's. Some days I wonder if Vero is just a female version of my man.

"That won't be necessary. I can handle him just fine."

"Yeah? Are you sure about that? He has that Hernandez temper. I should know, I have it too." My mind goes back

to the day of the party and my heart wants to spill over with emotion - Fabian has always been there for me in his way.

"Yeah..I've seen it."

"Pinche- Look, if he ever does anything to scare you, dial me. I will string his balls up to a tree, hermano or not." Her voice takes on a whole different octave, sounding like she's about to jump through the speaker.

Vero can be kind of scary. Images of her chasing her brother around with a knife held in the air float in my mind and I have to shake my head to get rid of it. She wouldn't, would she?

"No! He was - he was protecting me from someone. I love Fabian, I truly do. He's been there for me through ...everything. I don't know what I would do without him. I can't - I can't imagine life without him."

"Chica, you got it bad. How my asshole of a brother got someone like you, I'll never know. But I'm happy for you two. He loves you? He must if he's willing to take punches from mi esposo. Fabian never backs down from a fight. Well, except for that one time - but then the guy didn't show up around the neighborhood for a while. I always wondered about that -"

I have no idea what she's talking about as she continues to go down her own memory lane of her and her brother. Despite her calling him an asshole, I can tell they have a really good relationship together. Where does this leave me and my sisters? Will my mother ever let me talk to them again?

"- But anyway, enough about the past. How are you doing with everything that's happened? Do you need anything? What can I do to help?"

With the thought of not seeing my sisters and Fabian's sister trying to step up to the plate, my eyes start to tear up. I swore I would stop being like this over this situation. It's said and done - life has to move forward.

Wasn't it just the other day I wondered what it would be like to not be oppressed by my culture and religion anymore? I guess what they say is true - be careful what you ask for.

But looking over at Fabian measuring something in the house and jotting down notes on how he's going to fix it...I wouldn't change my decision for anything. I would always choose Fabian.

"Thank you, Vero."

"For what? I didn't even do anything yet."

"Just for being there for me, and for letting me love your brother."

Vero laughs and it almost bursts my eardrums. I can hear my brother in the background asking her what's going on and it kind of makes me want to smile.

"Chica, I don't know what you're smoking but I hope you're ready to be a Hernandez. When it comes to Fabian, I don't *'let' anything - Fabian is his own man who makes his own decisions. He's a good guy who always takes care of family. Keep him out of trouble and you two will be alright."*

Vero's easy acceptance of me into their family makes my heart hurt and want to burst at the same time. Saying our goodbyes, I end the call and turn to look at Fabian who has now removed his shirt to wipe the sweat off his face.

How did a girl like me get so lucky?

"Sakinah, get your ass on the bike and put on your helmet. My mother is probably already waiting for me at the doorway so she can throw a damn chancla at me for being late." Shaking my head at his dramatics, I shove the helmet on and start to buckle under my chin. Swinging my legs behind him, he starts the engine back up, strapping his own helmet on.

I hope we don't smell like exhaust fumes by the time we get there. His mother's neighborhood takes about a twenty-minute ride on his bike since Fabian is weaving in and out of traffic like a heathen, scaring the crap out of me. At least he has the decency to tap on my hand to let me know to hold on tighter because he's about to speed up.

My eyes start to notice the change in neighborhood scenery the closer we get. The houses become closer together, yards become smaller, the bars on the windows and doors become more prevalent. Fabian pulls up into the driveway of a very modest looking home and just like he said, his mother is already standing at the open screen door in her apron with what looks like a wooden spoon in her hand.

Swinging myself off the bike, I proceed to take off my helmet and leave it on the seat as Fabian does the same.

"¿Mira, mira quien viene? Why did you take so long? I'm here making comida for you and you want to make me wait? You don't even come over anymore. ¿Porque? ¿Quién es tu amiga? You did not tell me you were bringing una mujer." His mom is kind of scary, she reminds me of Vero when she's on a tirade. She continues to shake her wooden spoon at him but smiles at me. At least that's something.

I try to fix my hair since it's probably messed up from the helmet as Fabian starts responding back.

"Mamá, take it easy. La bendición. I'm here now aren't I? You should be happy I'm bringing someone over to see how good your comida tastes." My eyes widen when it looks like she wants to take her shoe off but thinks better of it since I'm standing right here.

"Que Dios te bendiga. You no answer my question, Hijo. ¿Quién es tu amiga?" Fabian opens his mouth to say something when another vehicle pulls up behind the bike. We all look over to see Vero practically hanging out of the passenger window yelling back.

"Mamá! Ella es su novia!" What?

I can see Akmal in the driver's seat as they pull into park.

"Su novia? Why do my children never tell me these things huh? They just come to mi casa and surprise, they're married? Sin respeto."

"Mamá, don't be like that. We respect you, that's why she's here today. I was going to introduce you to Sakinah."

"Oi, Sakinah? ¿Ella es su hermana, no? Explícamelo." The wooden spatula gets pointed at Akmal who just exited the car and is now leaning back with both hands up, palms out, in case Fabian's mother decides to go through with the threat.

"Mamá, let's all go inside so we can explain everything." She looks skeptical, mostly at Fabian, but allows him to usher her back inside.

"Oi! Fabian. ¿Quién es tu amiga? ¿Ella es tu esposa?" I didn't even notice Fabian's father standing at the doorway. He must have been watching all the dramatics outside on the front lawn this entire time, judging by the smirk on his face.

Some of the neighbors have conveniently come out to do things in their front yard too. I recognize the gossipers and eavesdroppers. We have them at our house as well - well, my old house.

"La bendición papá."

"Que Dios te bendiga, hija. Welcome back Akmal. You taking care of my daughter?"

"Yes, sir. Always."

"Papá! What kind of question is that?"

"The kind a father asks because he loves his hija." I watch as Vero hugs her father before we all trail behind and enter the home.

Akmal brings himself next to me and whispers, "Apa khabar? How are you? You holding up alright with every-thing that's happened?"

"Yeah, I guess. Fabian is helping a lot." My brother shoots a glare at Fabian and he smirks right back.

"If you need me for anything, just let me know."

"Thank you."

Once we pass the threshold of the screen door, we enter a cute little kitchen area. The smell of delicious food surrounds us as Fabian's mother starts pushing people to go sit down at the table. My culture being so deeply rooted has me following her into the kitchen to see if she needs any help. Vero is there already.

"Can I help you with anything?" I want to make a good impression and Vero knows it by the way she's trying to suppress a smile.

"Mi Mamá is a control freak. I just hang out to make her feel less alone. Ow!" Watching Vero get slapped upside the head shouldn't be as funny as it is.

"Mira tu boca! I've been doing this since before you were born. I don't need anyone breathing down my back."

"Mamá, why do you have to be so mean? You know I love you, I just want to hang out with you because I miss you." A wooden spoon gets swatted on her ass and Vero is laughing all the way to the table.

Now I find myself in an awkward position because I don't know what to do. It's the first time meeting her and I'm not sure how to talk to her now that we're alone.

"Are you Fabian's novia?"

"I'm not sure what that means."

"Mi hijo never brings a girl around. You are the first I've seen. But he's never mentioned you. I did not recognize you without that -" She waves her hand around her head to explain what she means. "- around your cabeza, the wrappy thing." My hand automatically goes to my head, wondering if maybe I should have worn it now.

"You look nicer like this. You have very beautiful hair." Feeling my face heat up, I mumble my thanks.

"Mamá! What are you saying to mi mujer? Be nice." Fabian comes up behind me and kisses me on the cheek right in front of his mother. *Oh my god. Is he allowed to do that?* I bury my face in his chest to hide my embarrassment. "What did you do Mamá?" I can feel his arms wrap around me in comfort.

"I did nothing. You're the one who brings home un mujer and don't tell anyone. How long have you two been together? Why don't you come over to mi casa anymore? Is it because of her? Why don't you just bring her here so I can see you too?"

"Relájate. She's here now isn't she?" Peeking sideways, I watch as his mother puts a hand over her chest as she takes a harsh inhale. What just happened?

"¿Está embarazada? You have un baby? Am I going to be an abuela? Are you married already? Did I miss it? Did you leave your poor Mamá y Papá out of your wedding?"

"Mamá, breathe. Let's just have this lunch and relax. Geez. Let us at least sit down first. So dramática."

"I wouldn't have to be dramática if you tell me these things! Okay, okay. Siéntate por favor. I will bring out the food."

"I can help you, if you want." Now I feel bad. I need to help somehow.

"No, no. Go sit down. I will bring out the food."

"You better just do what she says because she's a control freak." Something flies and hits Fabian. He doesn't even look to see what it is, only laughs and drags me by the hand to go sit down at the table.

Once seated, Fabian's father turns to me and stares at me intently. My hand starts to shake the longer I wait for him to say something.

"Oi, Fabian. ¿Ella es su hermana, no?" His hand points to Akmal on the other side of the table.

"Yes. Sakinah is Akmal's sister. Stop asking." His eyes haven't left mine though and I shoot a look at Akmal for some help. Vero isn't saying anything at all, just watching what's going down like it's her mini entertainment before lunch.

Before his dad can say anything, Fabian's mom starts to pile plates and plates of food on the table. Once everything and everyone is settled, the table says 'Buen provecho' and everyone starts digging in. Both Akmal and I whisper 'Bismillah' and start to do the same.

A few bites in and some of this stuff doesn't seem to agree with my stomach. So I try to find the ones that do.

"You okay?"

"Yeah. I guess I'm just not used to some of these things."

"Don't worry, you come around enough and you'll be eating everything she makes. She won't let you leave otherwise."

"What's wrong with mi comida?"

"Mamá! Nothing. I'm just telling her how good everything is. Geez." She narrows her eyes at him but continues to eat without further comment.

Some of this stuff really isn't agreeing with me, so I slowly stop eating. It feels like I'm just pushing my food around to make it look good but my stomach still says no.

"Fabian, go to the store." His mother's voice makes me snap my head up.

"Why? I'm still eating."

"Listen to your Mamá and go to the store. Su esposa está embarazada." Fabian's dad and Vero drop their utensils and look directly at me.

"I'm sorry?" The screech of Fabian's chair across the floor startles me as he kisses me on the cheek and runs out the door, Vero laughing right behind him.

"You're so dramática, Mamá."

"Oi, I know these things hija." Fabian's mother nods her head like it all makes sense, while I still have no idea what is going on.

"Yeah? Well, Akmal and I have an announcement to make." My brother chokes a little on his food with Vero's sudden change in demeanor. She slaps him on the back but ignores it and continues anyway.

"What is it now? Are you getting a divorce?"

"Papá, stop it. No, we're not getting a divorce. We're having a boy!"

"Dios Mio! I'm so excited for you! I'm going to have to make some blankets for the baby." Her mother literally starts crying and laughing at the same time with her hand over her heart while her dad is still looking at my brother skeptically.

"Papá! Be happy for me. You're going to be an abuelo."

"I am happy. I'm too young to be an abuelo. Fabian was enough." He laughs at that comment just as the roar of his bike comes back to the house.

Fabian comes stomping back into the house like he just ran back from wherever he just went off to. "Okay, Okay. I'm back. Sakinah, go to the bathroom."

"Huh? Why?" I stand up to see what he's talking about when he comes around the table and shoves a plastic bag full of boxes at me. *What is going on?* "What-"

"Go in the bathroom and pee on all of them."

"All of what? I don't even feel like I need to pee." He's pushing me and suddenly I find myself in a cozy little bathroom...with Fabian inside who's now shutting the door behind us.

"I'm not peeing in front of you!"

"I need you to pee on all the sticks. I didn't know which one to get so I got everything I saw."

"Why am I peeing on sticks?"

"Dammit Sakinah! Just do it!"

"Well, I'm not doing anything with you in here! Get out!"

"I need to see it to make sure."

"Make sure about what? What the hell are we talking about? What if I don't want to pee on anything? Fabian, what's going -"

He grabs my face and kisses me hard, passionately. If his plan was to calm me down, it's working because his warm body is pressing up against mine as I'm pushed against the sink of this bathroom.

"Sakinah."

"Yes?"

"I need you to pee on everything." Our warm breaths are caressing our lips with every word we say from how close we still are.

"What if I say no?" The knock on the door startles us both out of our moment together, the sound of Fabian's mother's voice makes me push him towards the door.

"What's going on in there? Fabian! Let her do it and come out here!"

"You're lucky this time. Pee on the sticks." His finger points at my chest where I'm still gripping tightly onto the plastic bag he shoved at me when he got back.

Watching him leave and shut the door, I sigh in relief. Turning, I untie the bag and look at what the boxes are inside, my eyes widening when I start to read the print.

"Tu esposa inside?" Great, now his dad is right outside too.

"Yeah."

"Does she know that?" Vero's laughing and I stop opening the box to listen intently.

"Not yet."

Taking a deep breath, I start to open each box and read the directions. My hands are shaking a little bit and my mind feels lightheaded. I mean, I should have expected it but it never crossed my mind. It was stupid of me. I should have been more careful.

I almost don't have enough pee for all of the damn pregnancy tests Fabian brought back. Why does anyone need this many? Washing up, I wring my hands nervously and start to wonder if I should wait outside instead of staring at the sticks as each second passes.

I should go outside.

Opening the door, all I see is Fabian's back. He turns to look at me with a big 'ol smile on his face.

"Why are you smiling like that?"

"Because I knocked up my wife."

"I'm not your wife."

"You were going to be anyway, so might as well get used to calling me husband, *wife*."

"Oi! Am I going to be an abuela again? You *did* get married?! Why you not invite your Mamá y Papá to your wedding? Fabian!"

"You didn't miss it Mamá, I'm going to marry her as soon as I find out what that stick says. She's already mi esposa anyway."

"We're getting married?"

"Yeah, we are. I'm booking a flight after we go back home."

"Where are you going?" His mother's voice sounds a little frantic. I'm feeling a little frantic too with how fast every-thing's going - but a little excited as well.

"It's been ten minutes already." Vero's voice brings me back to the present and my heart starts racing as I run back to the restroom to see the results.

There are seven sticks all lined up across the sink and my hands try to match the directions to the brand of each stick. Why can't they all just read the same? Why must it be so damn complicated?

Vero pushes her brother aside as they bicker about who should be in here with me but my mind is concentrating so hard on the fine print of these directions my eyes are about to cross.

"Sakinah."

"I'm not sure which one goes with this one."

"Sakinah."

"Huh?"

"You're pregnant." My hand drops the paper as I stare at Vero through tear blurred eyes.

"Are you sure?"

"Yeah, I've taken a few of these myself." She laughs as she rubs her small growing belly and I'm reminded of the day they made the announcement at home.

No longer my home.

"It's okay, it's okay." She hugs me and my tears fall quickly turning into sobs.

"What did you do to her?"

"I didn't do anything Fabian. Relax. Let her feel whatever she needs to feel right now."

"Sakinah, are you okay?"

Lifting my head from Vero's chest, I turn and throw myself into Fabian's arms.

"What's wrong?" Wiping my eyes against his shirt, I shake my head.

"Nothing's wrong. I'm just...happy and sad."

"She's pregnant." Vero supplies and nods since I seem to have become an emotional mess.

"You're crying because you're pregnant with my baby?"

Lifting my head up, I slap Fabian in the chest to make him shut up.

"Not everything is about you, you asshole. I'm crying because I'm happy that I'm pregnant, but I can't celebrate it with my family because - because -"

Fabian leans down towards my face and gives me a soft smile. "You don't have to worry about that Sakinah. We're a family now. And mi Mamá y Papá, and I guess we'll let Vero come too. Ow! What did you hit me for?"

Vero laughs and walks out the overcrowded bathroom as Fabian continues to rub the back of his head, trying to suppress his own laugh. His attempt to lighten the mood works and I hug him tightly.

I'm pregnant. He's right. We're a family now. What was he saying earlier about booking flights?

Fabian is pulled off me as his mother looks at me with tears in her eyes. "¿Está embarazada? I'm going to be an abuela again, sí? Oi! I'm so feliz!" She hugs me so hard that I can barely breathe.

"Fabian!"

"Sí Papá."

"You bring home your first girl and you're already married and starting a family? How come you don't tell me this when I was helping you move? Is that why you buy the house?"

My mind starts to click things together as Fabian looks over at me with a wink and a smile, his hands doing something on his phone.

"Familia, pack your bags for a few days. Yeah, you too Akmal."

"¿Porque?"

"Why? What's going on?"

"Tu Papá better be your best man." I'm standing here trying to figure out why Fabian's dad is talking about himself in third person when -

"For the wedding. We're going to Vegas."

"Dios Mio. I need to find my nice dress."

"Hermano! That's what I'm talking about! Come on Akmal, we have to go home and pack!"

My eyes tear up again and I'm starting to wonder if it's from the hormones or if I've always just been a crybaby on the inside.

Fabian comes over and cradles my face in his warm hands, wiping away the tears that have escaped. "You're stuck with me now."

"Asshole, you're stuck with me. Are you sure you want to be?"

"Sakinah, I was sure the moment you slapped my face." A laugh bursts out of me as Fabian wraps his arms around me and lifts me up for a kiss.

Chapter Seventeen

FABIAN

The flight to Vegas is quick and simple. Vero isn't too far along yet and Sakinah hasn't shown any other signs or symptoms of her pregnancy that would prevent her from sitting on a plane. My parents are a ball of nerves as they haven't traveled much. I figured this little trip would be a nice gift for them as well. They've worked hard taking care of us and bringing us up right; They deserve a little vacation. I called Omar to let him know what's happening and for him to keep in contact with me in case we pick up another contract.

"I'll be right back."

I look at my soon-to-be wife, seeing if anything is wrong but she looks alright. I should ask her anyway. "Do you need me?"

"No, I'm just going to the restroom."

"Maybe I need to make sure my pregnant wife is okay."

"Fabian, you're too much." She says this but I'm already following her out of my seat and she's not even stopping me.

The flight attendants are on the other side of the plane and the plane itself is only half full since we booked a flight on a random weekday.

When Sakinah opens the restroom door, I usher both of us inside, closing and locking it.

"Fabian! What are you doing?"

"Taking care of my pregnant wife, what do you think I'm doing?"

"I just need to check myself a little bit. You didn't have to follow me."

"I'm always going to follow you Sakinah, you're mine and I always take care of what's mine."

"How are you going to take care of me? We're in this small bathroom." This room *is* fucking small.

"Well, my pregnant wife was looking a little stressed. Maybe I can help with that."

"Oh yeah?" Her cute little smile graces her face and I know I got her. Ever since the blow out with her family, Sakinah has been slowly dressing a little differently, not wrapping her head as much. And as beautiful as she is, it just makes me even hornier every time I see her.

Like right now, for instance.

Leaning into her, I start to nip on her earlobe. She loves that shit, always starts to squirm. "Are you wearing any panties, Sakinah?"

"Fabian!" My hands are already going up her skirt and can feel the wetness soaking through the panties that shouldn't be there. I'm going to have to make sure she stops wearing it when we go places together.

Pushing the crotch aside, my fingers start to play with her folds as Sakinah's fingernails start digging into my shoulder and up my neck sending shivers down my spine. She's become a little more aggressive and brazen lately, making me excited to see how far she'll let me push her. Not that she really has much of a choice anyway because my dick is going in her one way or another.

It's a good thing women's panties are thin as hell because I give it a good tug and rip these off her, sticking it into my back pocket as my lips press against hers to distract her from yelling at me.

"Fabian."

"Don't worry, I'll take care of you. Open your legs for me." She wraps one of her legs around me as my hands start to unbuckle my jeans. Unlike some people, I come prepared with no boxers to hold me back. I can feel my dick spring out and slap her in the pussy, making her whimper against my mouth.

Liking the sound, I grab my dick and slap her a few more times, rubbing the head of my cock against her wet opening but not pushing it too far in yet. Sakinah likes it when I tease her despite how hard her nails are digging into me right now, she's just afraid to admit it. It's a good thing her husband is good at reading her body.

I've never had a chance to join the mile high club, I guess today is going to be the day as I slowly shove the head of my dick inside of her tight little pussy. She moans into my mouth and my hands lift her ass to bring her up higher, making her other leg wrap around me for leverage. The sink in this damn plane is tiny as hell but so is Sakinah so I place her on the edge of it as I start to pound into her.

Her moans and whimpers are getting louder. Sticking my tongue inside of her mouth, I try to mask the sound. Wouldn't be good to be caught fucking my wife in public places, not that it would stop me anyway.

When her breaths start to come out in pants, I whisper against her lips. "You're so fucking wet down there. Were you waiting for me to fuck you?"

"Maybe."

"Maybe?" My hips thrust into her even harder for the simple fact that she always makes me chase her, the little brat. "Maybe next time I should just fuck you in front of everyone, so you can remember to tell me instead of making me follow you around and spreading your legs when I catch you."

"I like it when you make me spread my legs." I groan into her neck as my hands start to squeeze between us and play with her pussy. The good thing about everything that's happened is that I don't have to fucking pull out anymore.

She's the only girl I've ever gone bareback with and I don't think I could ever go back. Sakinah is just going to have to stay knocked up.

Thinking about her stomach swollen with my kids makes my balls tighten as I grab her ass even harder, slamming into her while my thumb and forefinger start to pinch her swollen clit. Knowing her body the way I do now, I can tell she's about to cum on my dick when I hear her try to moan my name in that way she does. My mouth covers hers again to stifle the sound before she can cry out as she orgasms and starts milking my dick for all it's worth, making me cum right after her.

Still thrusting into her, making sure none of it comes out, someone knocks on the door ruining our beautiful moment.

"Cabrón! I need to go pee. Hurry up in there and make sure my sister looks good before you let her out."

Sakinah giggles against my lips as I let her legs down, my dick slipping out of her. I can't help but keep touching her as my fingers push my cum back inside her pussy as it tries to go down her legs.

"You're so dirty, Sakinah. You're going to sit next to me and feel this between your legs until we land. When we get to the hotel, I'm going to fill you up some more."

"Fucker! I need to go pee, I'm pregnant and shit!"

I chuckle as Sakinah's eyes widen, moving her off the sink so I can wash my hands. Fixing our clothes, we both exit out the little restroom door as my sister stands there with her arms crossed.

"Relájate, you didn't pee on yourself. You're fine." I dodge Vero's punch as she pushes us out of the way and slams the door shut. *Sheesh.* Hopefully, Sakinah doesn't get like that the further her pregnancy goes.

Then again, I'm usually surrounded by sassy women anyway, I should be used to it by now. The flight goes for another thirty or so minutes before the captain tells us we've reached our destination. We land during the hotter seasons and we're already sweating before we can even leave the damn airport.

I had booked separate rooms for my parents and for Vero and her husband so I can have time to spend with my girl before the wedding.

I'm glad we're doing Vegas. I need her to be my wife like yesterday. Vero and I had a discussion prior to boarding the plane - She's going to go out with Akmal to find the rings once we split up while I help my girl settle in the room.

We have a day to relax before the wedding happens tomorrow. I wonder if we'll get an Elvis impersonator to marry us? Doesn't matter, as long as I tie this woman to my side forever. Who knew Fabian Hernandez would be settling down. I didn't. Not until Sakinah came into my life.

"I've never been to Vegas before."

"Yeah? Well we're here now. Soon you're going to be Mrs. Hernandez. Are you ready for it?" She turns to me once we get inside our hotel room door and gives me the brightest smile I've ever seen on her. It makes my pride glow, knowing I put it there.

"Yeah, I am."

<hr>

"Fabian, stop. It's too much."

"It's not. You can take it."

"Oh my god."

Sakinah is practically bent in two on her back as I fuck her harder and harder like I'm punishing my dick for wanting her so damn much.

"It's not my fault you make me this way."

"What fucking way? You barely let me sleep at all last night."

Slowing my thrusts down, my thumb starts to rub her clit in slow circles, watching her breasts rise and fall with her breathing. Her mouth parts and bring one of my legs up to help me fuck her harder into the mattress. She doesn't disappoint as she cries out while squeezing my dick. Being the bastard I am, I pull out and rub my cum all over her pussy, shooting some on her stomach, watching it glisten in the sunlight that's streaming in from the window as it coats her.

She's so fucking beautiful like this.

Plus, we have to go shower anyway and get ready for this wedding.

Slapping her ass, she tries to kick me but I jump out of the way anticipating it. "Come on, let's go shower and get this day over with so I can bring you back and fuck you again."

"Fabian! I'm going to come back and take a damn nap."

"You can try. You don't have to be awake for me to stick it in you. Just keep sleeping."

She slaps my chest with a cute little snarl as we both get into the biggest shower I've ever been in. *Good, plenty of damn room.* Turning the water on, I watch as Sakinah bends over to look at the little hotel shampoos and my hand grabs her ass from behind. She really does make it too easy.

"Dammit Fabian! We need to get ready!"

"Fine, fine. Relax, don't get so mad. We have plenty of time."

"We do not, you horny asshole. You don't have to wash long hair." Grabbing the little shampoo bottle from her hand, I push her under the water to wet her hair as she continues to cuss at me lovingly the way she always does.

Moving her body out of the water, I squirt some of the girly smelling shit into my hands and lather her hair. She stops squirming and calms down just like I knew she would, letting me wash her hair for her.

Sadly, she didn't let me sneak a quickie in as we both get out of the shower and dry ourselves off. I'm just walking out of the restroom when there's a knock on the door. Opening it I see Vero and Akmal all ready. Damn, what time is it?

"Why aren't you dressed? You're going to be late to your own damn wedding." Vero pushes me aside as she walks towards Sakinah and ushers her to the other side of the room to help her do whatever it is girls do to get ready.

I'm left standing here with Akmal and none of us want to be the first to talk. It's been a little strained between us since the whole 'I fell in love with your sister' thing.

"Look man, I'm not sorry about what happened before."

"I'm not sorry about falling in love with your sister."

"Yeah, I can see that. Just - Just take care of her alright? Make sure she's happy. We're all she's got now."

"Of course. I wouldn't have it any other way. She makes me happy, man. I've made it my mission to keep her as happy as she makes me." Akmal puts his hand on my shoulder and nods. I think we've come to an agreement on this at least.

"Alright, well, unless you're getting married naked, I think you should start getting dressed. You got about fifteen minutes."

"Fabian! Get your ass dressed, I'm not marrying you naked!"

"Ah... my lovely wife calls. Alright, let's do this."

Chapter Eighteen

SAKINAH

Is this really happening? I'm walking down this short aisle with Akmal on my arm. I'm sad that the rest of my family can't be here but at least I have support from my new family. The moment I see Fabian standing near the Elvis impersonator, is the moment my eyes start burning with accumulating tears but I try to blink it back so it doesn't streak my mascara down my face. Vero worked her magic on me and I couldn't even recognize myself in the mirror.

Not wanting to choose favorites, Fabian ended up telling both his dad and Akmal that they're his best men. I did the same with Vero and my future mother in law. I don't remember anything the Elvis guy said because he was trying too hard with the accent but time stood still as Fabian put the most beautiful ring on my finger. *When did he even have time to get this?*

We seal our marriage with a kiss and grab the marriage certificate before we leave the building. The parents tell us they're splitting and going to have fun at the casinos leaving Akmal and Vero the only people left with us.

"You want to hit up the buffet?"

"Didn't I just see you sneak something into your mouth when the Elvis guy was talking?" Vero shoots Fabian a look that would make a normal man cringe.

"I'm pregnant you idiot. I'm fucking hungry. Akmal, take me to a buffet please!"

"Relájate. We'll all go eat, I need to feed my pregnant *wife* anyway."

"How sweet." Vero makes a gagging sound and I laugh my ass off.

Vegas has so many buffets to choose from, I'm surprised Vero can even make a decision. But she does and we all sit down at a booth together once everyone gets their food.

"So, Sakinah, what are you planning to do after you finish school? This is your last semester right?" Vero is making heart eyes at all the plates in front of her as she asks me this.

"Yeah, it is. I haven't thought about it yet."

"You're smart, you'll figure it out." Akmal, always so supportive.

"Why don't you go into structural designs? That project you and Jason were working on was pretty solid."

"But you made that little model."

"Yeah, from *your* notes."

"Fabian made a model of something?"

"Just keep eating, Vero." He flips his sister off and I try not to laugh. Their personalities are contagious.

"I don't know..."

"You know, my buddy Omar and I have talked about starting a business together. Waiting on these contracts can be frustrating because there's never a set period of time that'll be a dry season. That's why we take up private contractor work in the meantime. I've built sheds and extra garages in some of the nicer neighborhoods. Maybe we should start something and you can help us with the design work."

"Really? I don't even know the first thing about that stuff."

"Yes you do. You're smart Sakinah. Don't sell yourself short. I've seen the kind of notes and stuff you write down on your engineering homework. That shit is way out of my league. But together, we might be able to do something good." My cheeks feel hot from all his compliments in front of his sister and my brother. He seems so confident in me. "Plus, I want my wife to be by my side anyway. Can't have other men around her when I'm not there to make my claim, you know?"

"Omar sounds like a guy's name."

"Yeah, but he's an old fucker. We've worked together forever, I trust him. If it makes you feel any better, you can offer something up to that Jason kid, since you guys work well together. He's a good follower and keeps out of trouble."

We continue to eat and talk about random things but my mind is trying to organize everything Fabian is throwing at me. Would it work? Can we start a business together? Me designing blueprints while Fabian puts them together. The thought of Fabian working shirtless around our house gives me tingles. I probably should be there with him so no one tries to take my man from under my nose.

Vero comes back with her fifth plate of food when I finally ask myself: what do I have to lose?

The next day in Vegas was nice, hanging by the pool and walking along the strip. A honeymoon filled with lights and laughter surrounded by great company. I'm almost sad to have to say goodbye to it. But reality calls and time moves forward.

Coming back home as Mrs. Hernandez is weird but exhilarating. My cheesy husband even insisted on carrying me over the threshold, even though we've already been living together for a while.

"Why do you need to carry me over the door? We've been walking over it every damn day."

"Sakinah, quit being a brat and just let me do this."

"Why? I'm not a brat." Standing on the sidewalk in front of our home, I jump when I see Fabian start coming at me from around the driver side of the car, leaving our bags behind. I only make it a few feet when he lifts me up and runs up our stairs, unlocks the door, walks in and drops me unceremoniously onto the couch before heading back outside.

"Asshole."

"I can still hear you!"

"Good!" Getting off the couch, I start to walk towards the door to help grab the bags and bring them into the bedroom to unpack.

Fabian smacks me on the ass when I'm not looking and the sting of the hit still lingers as I stick my tongue out at him.

"You keep that up Sakinah. I know what you want."

"You don't know anything, Mister Hernandez."

"Oh, I believe I do, Mrs. Hernandez."

The asshole didn't let me sleep that night either.

———

Classes started back up quickly, the countdown to graduation getting closer and closer. Jason and I had some classes together and I did in fact bring up the business idea to him.

"Hell yeah! I'd love to work with you guys. Fabian is a genius with his hands. The precision of that model was out of this world. Just tell me when."

"I'll let my husband know you're on board."

"Woah! Your husband? I just saw you guys like a month ago?"

"Yeah... it's a long story."

"Sakinah."

"Huh?"

"Baby, I've been trying to get your attention for the last few minutes. What are you thinking about?" My hand rubs my stomach unconsciously as I look at my husband standing in the kitchen shirtless. I always seem to find myself sitting down somewhere as my thoughts become scattered.

"About graduation and the business."

"Don't worry about it. I'll handle all the details. All you need to bring is your brilliant mind and that puppy that follows you around - what's his face."

"You're such an asshole. You know his name is Jason."

"Yeah, that guy." Throwing a cloth napkin from the table at him, it falls short making me laugh and almost peeing myself. This pregnancy stuff is no joke.

"Sakinah, if you wanted me to bend over for you, all you had to do was ask nicely. Don't go throwing shit in the house."

"I don't think I'm going to walk for graduation."

"Why not?"

"Look at me, I'll be showing even more by then."

"I can barely see anything. Maybe I need to fill you up some more to make sure you're really pregnant."

"Fabian!"

"Damn woman, relájate. It will be fine. Walk up there proudly. I'll be waiting to catch you in case you tumble." How does this man always know the right things to say to make me feel better?

I just kick my feet up on the other chair when there's a knock at the door.

"That must be Omar, I invited him over."

"Why didn't you tell me? I could have at least put something decent on."

"Baby, you look beautiful. Stop. He's just coming in to help me do some stuff in the laundry room I'm setting up. Plus, I haven't seen his ass since the last contract. It'll be good for you to get to know him too since we'll be business partners and all that."

Taking my feet off the chair, I stand up at the exact moment an older middle aged gentleman comes in with a friendly bearded smile.

"Omar! This is my wife, Sakinah."

"I've heard so much about you, glad he wasn't just lying out of his ass." He sticks his hands out to me in greeting. His handshake is firm but kind - and also really dry. *Someone give this man some lotion.*

"Really? What has my beloved *husband* been saying about me exactly?" I side-eye Fabian but all he does is blow a kiss at me.

"It really wasn't what he said, but how he talked about you. I couldn't get him to shut up and get to the damn point of his phone calls. I've never seen Fabian worked up over a girl before."

"Knowing my husband, I'm not sure if I should be flattered or if I should kick his ass." Omar's booming laugh shakes the windows and makes me want to laugh too. His sun weathered face is charming and the way his shoulder shakes is something else.

"Alright. I see why he loves you. You make sure you keep that boy in line."

"You know, I'm standing right fucking here."

"Yeah well what you need to be doing is telling me what the hell you called me over for. What are we doing today?"

"Well, I need to expand this laundry area and add some cabinets on top. I also called you over because we need to follow through on that business venture we've always talked about."

"Yeah, you're down for it? When are we doing this?" Fabian looks at me and then at my stomach and back at Omar.

"Like right fucking now."

Chapter Nineteen

FABIAN

I was able to convince Sakinah to walk for graduation. No one could even tell she was pregnant under the graduation gown. She cried when she made it back to my arms, I was so proud of her. Hopefully, the baby gets her smarts and my good looks. I bet the baby is going to be a boy, I can feel it. Plus every time she's asleep and I tell him to kick me if he's a boy, he does - so there's that. Already a good kid that listens to his dad.

Omar and I got the business loan and started creating our company: C&H Construction. Some of the guys from the old work site agreed to come on temporarily to help us get a good foothold on our clientele.

Sakinah and Jason work the office we leased, going over ideas on blueprints and whatever else they do in the office. Sakinah is really good with organization, so I leave that shit up to her. Omar's taking a liking to her, always hanging out and dodging work when Sakinah brings food over. Fucker thinks I don't see it. Good thing I'm always hanging out too when she brings food to work.

Sakinah has started to glow even more than she usually does the farther along she gets with this pregnancy. She decided she didn't want to know the gender, so who am I to say anything. I just need the baby to get here so I can put another one in her. I'm excited to be a father. My mother is the most excited of all, coming over and bringing trays and trays of food. You swear she thinks we're both going to starve now that Sakinah is carrying a baby.

"Do I look big in this?" Oh hell no I'm not falling for that shit. Coming up behind her, I hold her and kiss her head.

"You look beautiful, like the woman who's bringing the miracle of life into the world." She looks over her shoulder with a lifted eyebrow. *What?*

"You're just lucky your tongue game is good."

"Yeah? Do you need me to convince you again? You look skeptical. I don't like my wife doubting me."

"Fabian! I mean your way with words."

"I can speak words down there too."

"How can you still love my body when I can barely see my own feet."

"You want me to lick your feet?"

"Dammit, Fabian! Be serious!"

"I am! You look fine. Stop acting like that. I'd love you even if you're spitting out our twentieth kid."

"Twenty kids?!"

The first item off the dresser flies at my head but I managed to duck in time. Damn, it's a good thing I know how to fix drywall because at this rate, there's going to be a million holes.

———

ATSUKO AND VERO WERE KIND ENOUGH TO START buddying up with Sakinah for maternity clothes shopping. I'm glad Sakinah has found new sisters she can hang out with - of course it's not the same as her own but still good.

The boys and I are hanging out at home, checking out the added laundry room Omar and I completed when the sound of the girl's giggles come in through the front door.

"It is so cute! You should just buy everything in neutral colors so you won't have to take anything back!" My sister's voice is, of course, the loudest one.

"That's so smart!"

"Well men, looks like the hens are back in the hen house."

"Cabrón, who are you calling hens? What have you boys been up to since we were out?" Why does she have to be like that? This isn't even her house anyway.

"We painted the damn baby room." The project went fast with two other guys helping me. Sakinah asked me to paint it this weird shade of green and yellow, but what do I know? The baby probably doesn't even care what color the damn room is.

"Oh my god! You did?"

I catch my wife before she can take a tumble and pick her up for a kiss. This pregnancy has made her clumsier but it gives me an excuse to touch her more - and for her to miss when she tries to kick me when she's pissed.

"Of course. Ask and you shall receive. What kind of husband would I be if I didn't do all the hard work?"

"You guys make me sick."

"Vero, be nice." That's right Akmal. You tell her.

"He's mi hermano, I don't need to be nice."

"How you handle her on a daily basis, I will never know, Akmal."

"I don't know either. Ow!" Damn, mi hermana has become even more vicious with this pregnancy.

"You're supposed to back me up."

"Vero, you can be a bit much sometimes." Finally a woman with some sense.

"You too Atsuko?"

"Stop it you two. She's not any better." Damn Mat, you just stuck your foot in your mouth and buried yourself.

"What is that supposed to mean Mat?" Atsuko looks like she's about to withhold sex for the next damn month. I feel sorry for him.

"Nothing!"

I better save these fuckers before they dig their hole any deeper.

"He means that all you hens together start cackling like crazy and it drives the roosters up the wall." Dodging my sister's attempt at throwing a pillow from the couch at my head, I laugh as I go into the kitchen and bring out some snacks.

These crazy pregnant women always calm down when there's snacks.

We all sit down in the living room and start to chat about random things. But the name that comes out of Akmal's mouth makes me tense up.

"What did you just say?"

"That, um, my mother got a recording in the mail and she finally found out the kind of man Amir is." His eyes dart to mine and then to Mat's but the girls don't notice since they're all currently stuffing their faces.

Shit, just hearing that fucker's name makes my blood boil. While the girls were out one day, the boys and I hunted down that asshole. Well, it was more of me hunting his ass down while I dragged Akmal and Mat with me. They didn't believe me when I told them. So what if I have a reputation for being hot tempered? I know what I saw - the way Sakinah looked at me that day will be ingrained into my mind like a damn scar.

"Bisaam was able to set something up for us. He told Amir to meet him up at this place for a get together - like a boys night." It's a good thing Bisaam is a mutual friend or else this wouldn't have worked. Well, I would have made it happen anyway but there's less police involvement this way.

"You think he took the bait?" Mat is already looking through his phone to make sure it goes on record when that fucker gets here.

"Yeah. He likes that kind of uppity shit - going to parties so he can show off something about himself. I never liked him, that's why I never let him come over to my parents' house. But I guess he must have convinced my mother somehow. She invited the whole damn city for our wedding."

"I don't care how that asshole got into the family, he just needs to stay the fuck away because he's not touching another woman in our family like that again." If I had it my way, he would never be allowed to breathe again.

"Shit, I can't believe he hit my sister, man. She's so damn quiet." I chuckle under my breath because he has no idea what Sakinah is like when she lets her filter down.

"Shh.. I think he's coming." We're hiding in the back of an alley by some dumpsters - I know, typical like a bunch of thugs - but we have to get him where no one can see.

His shiny BMW pulls up the back towards us thinking there's a party. It's a deserted building but with enough pedestrian traffic going by with the other buildings that it doesn't rouse that much suspicion.

The moment he opens his door is the moment I come up behind him and use his body to slam the door shut.

"The fuck?" His eyes widen when he sees me and my boys behind me.

"Glad we can meet again, asshole."

"Shit, you already got the bitch, what more do you want?" Punching him in the face, his head whips to the side, blood trailing out the corner of his mouth.

"Excuse me?" I bet my brother-in-law believes me now.

"Fuck, Akmal, I didn't see you there. Nah, I didn't mean anything by it." Yet the words just came out of his damn mouth.

"Like you didn't mean to slap my fucking sister in the face?" Yeah, that's right Amir, look scared because we all know who's the little bitch here. Can't hide behind your lies anymore.

His face goes from pretending to be innocent to something ugly.

"She kept talking back, I was trying to get her to stop. She brought it on to herself." I throw Amir towards Akmal as he lands a punch or two in his gut. I would kill this fucker if I didn't think Sakinah would bury me for getting locked up. Can't leave my pregnant woman alone like that.

Mat's been recording this whole shit, his job is to edit us all out and just get Amir admitting what he did so we can have evidence on him.

I let Akmal get his beating in a few more times before I pull the rich fucker off the ground and slam him onto the hood of his car - It needs a little dent or two anyway, shit has no personality just like its owner.

His head must have been knocked around a little too much because he starts talking right out of his ass the more punches we land in him.

"You can fucking have that whore! I was going to keep her in line and fucking knock her around anyway to get your spawn out of her before I even stick my dick inside that used cunt." Did I think I was pissed? It was nothing like Mat blowing up and knocking this fucker's teeth out after he pulled me off him.

Both Akmal and I just stepped back as Mat went to town, almost killing the bastard. We were able to pull him off in time, feeling Amir's pulse to make sure he's still breathing. It was later, after we left, that Mat admitted what happened to his parents and the hair trigger he has about guys who beat on women.

Damn, if I ever need some guys to back me up, I'm glad I don't have to look far.

"Yeah? And what did your mom do?" Mat's voice pulls me out of the memory and back into the conversation. The guys are trying to play it cool.

"Well, she was fucking pissed. She started going off on his mother until she found out he was in the hospital. It only toned down her anger a little bit because she felt bad but she's spreading the news about how he tried to trick her into marrying one of her daughters off to him."

"I don't care. I'm glad he got what was coming to him. Fabian is my husband. I would have never chosen Amir even if Fabian wasn't in the picture." Sakinah is pissed as she talks about him.

She stands up and tries to leave the room but I grab her arm and pull her onto my lap and hold her. She doesn't need any more stress, it's not good for the baby.

"Damn fucking straight. My woman is smart, it's what I love about her." Kissing her on the cheek, she calms down a little bit.

My eyes go to Mat and Akmal and they both subtly nod in understanding. What happened that day is a secret that will go to our grave.

Epilogue

SAKINAH

"Alex, get away from that!" Oh, the little rascal!

"Alright little man, up you go!" Fabian always amazes me with his timing. It's like he has daddy intuition when his son is up to trouble. I guess the fruit doesn't fall too far from the tree, so he would have a good radar. He lifts our son in his arms and the boy squeals in delight. He loves his daddy. I love his daddy too as I watch him blow on our son's tummy, making him squirm.

At two years old, Fabian's little mini-me, Alejandro, is giving me a run for my money - making me chase him all over the place. Every time it gets quiet, I get scared. Every time I catch him doing something and start to get mad, his little smile and dimples melt my damn heart.

He's got his daddy's smirk too. We named him after his grandfather who started tearing up when we told him the news.

Fabian and Omar built a little playground in the back-yard but Alex is still much too small for some of the things. It doesn't stop him from trying. When the girls come over for playdates, Dawn and Yaakob love running around and playing on the swings since they're about four months older than Alex. Who knew that a few months would make such a big difference in kids? But little Alex always tries his best to catch up.

Akmal and Vero decided on a more traditional name for their son, Yaakob while Mat and Atsuko were tired of complicated names and went for something much more simple.

My mother-in-law was so ecstatic about the kids that she started crocheting little baby clothes and blankets all over the place. I'm glad Alex grew up enough to not get his finger stuck between the yarn. His little toddler bed is full of blankets, I can't even keep track of how many since he drags some of his favorites around.

Following the boys inside the backdoor, I waddle myself over the kitchen table and grab a bottle of water.

"Sakinah, baby, sit down. You don't need to be chasing this little guy around. I got him."

"Okay." Finishing the bottle of water, I put it down on the tabletop next to the baby monitor. Little Fernando is still sleeping in his crib soundly - thank goodness he's a deep sleeper.

Rubbing my hand over my belly, I kick my feet up on the other chair to give my ankles some rest. I can hear the boys in the living room playing with toys and so I bring my feet down and stand up to get some food ready. Fabian's sons eat just as much as he does, I don't know how they do it or where they put it. Good thing I love to cook, so I don't mind too much.

Taking out some of the pots and pans, I set the ingredients out for a simple spaghetti meal when the doorbell rings - Fabian had installed one a few years back.

"I got it." Fabian never wants me to do anything but stay barefoot and pregnant.

Continuing what I started, my ears listen intently in case one of the babies needs me. Now that I think of it, I might as well grab the baby monitor and bring it into the kitchen. Walking towards the table to do just that, I hear a voice I never thought I'd hear again.

"Is Sakinah here? Oh-"

"What do you want? You're not going near her."

"She's here to apologize for what she did. Tell him la, I want to see my daughter again." Walao eh - oh my god - Is that my dad?

My eyes start to tear up as I turn off the stove and waddle towards Fabian who is standing at the front door, holding Alex in his arms. My husband does not look happy to see my family and I don't blame him.

"I was trying to bring happiness to my daughter by finding her a husband so she can have her own family. I did not know about Amir and his reputation until later. I did not know."

"That doesn't negate the fact that you - her mother - was abusing my wife when you were trying to get her to marry that good-for-nothing bast -" Fabian stops his tirade just in time as he looks to our son in his arms. It's a heated subject that he never wants to bring up, choosing instead to concentrate on giving his family the best life he can.

"Ibu, bapa." My father's eyes widen and my mother's hand goes to her heart when they see my stomach peeking out from behind my husband. Little Fernando takes that exact moment to start crying and I turn to go to the kid's room to get him. When I return, Fabian still hasn't let my parents through the door yet. I'm not sure what I should do.

"Sakinah. I didn't know." She makes this sniffing noise while crossing her arms almost side-eyeing me. "I made a mistake, Sakinah."

"It doesn't matter, Ibu. Even if you did, I still love Fabian. I do not want anyone else."

"Your Ibu means well. She can get carried away sometimes. I am glad you are doing okay. These are all your babies?"

Rocking Fernando on my hip, he hides his face into my chest, not recognizing them. I can see the hurt in my Bapa's eyes but they did this to themselves. Though my mind tells me this, I don't know why my chest and heart still feels so heavy with guilt.

The sound of another car pulls up and my eyes leave my parents standing there awkwardly when I see Vero,

Akmal and Yaakob come out. When my parents turn to look at our new visitors, my eyes go to Fabian, unsure of what I should do.

"You tell me what you want, baby. I'm here for you, not for them." That's the hard part, I don't know what I want - I don't know what to do. Hugging him and squishing our babies in between, I take a deep breath, taking in his comfort and strength.

"Bapa, Ibu, what are you doing here? Don't upset Sakinah, it's not good for the baby." My brave brother gives our mother a stern look as he nudges her with his hand. Vero is curling her lip at Ibu while holding Yaakob on her hip.

"Aiyoh, okay, I made a mistake Sakinah." It doesn't sound like she means it at all. My mother will always be my mother, too prideful to apologize for what she did.

Bapa tries to fix her apology by inserting himself after her. "Sorry for all the trouble. We won't make the same mistake again." Ibu stares at him like it was his fault to begin with. I just can't with her.

But my deeply ingrained manners refuse to let them stand out there any longer. "Okay, come in and sit down everyone." Poor Akmal and Vero are still staring daggers at Ibu. She has to feel the tension around her.

Leading by example, I turn and put Fernando on the floor as Fabian does the same with Alex. Yaakob is already squealing as he runs past his grandparents to go play with his cousins. My brother ushers our parents towards the kitchen table and Vero comes to help me finish the spaghetti I put on hold. I was going to make extra anyway so there will be plenty for our last minute guests - Fabian will just have to go into the pantry for a snack if he's still hungry.

Awkward silence and small talk ensue as Vero and I start serving up plates and making sure the kids have their share at their little table in the corner next to us.

Murmurs of 'bismillah' and 'buen provecho' go around the table and we all start to eat in awkward silence.

"So you have another baby coming huh? Is it going to be a boy? Or a girl? Is it twins? Triplets?" I choke on my spaghetti as Fabian laughs out loud making the kids laugh and squeal. Vero is slapping my back as Akmal tries to hold back a grin.

My mother continues her interrogation of my life like nothing ever happened.

We continue to eat, the mood lightened by my Ibu's outburst. My gaze sweeps over the table and watch as all of us find ourselves smiling at each other and conversing more easily, the tension from earlier slowly melting away.

My heart feels so full that my eyes start to tear up again. *These damn hormones are going to kill me.* Fabian grabs my hand under the table and gives me a smirk and a wink reminding me that life is what we make of it.

I was always scared to find out what the consequences of our actions held, how it would blow up in our faces. The cultural obligations and fear of the unknown crippling what our future had in store for us. It was Fabian's strength that got me through my toughest times, when my mind was starting to fall into the depression of our consequences. And it was Fabian and the children who kept me going even when my family issues seemed like there was no way of fixing itself.

But here we sit surrounded by loved ones, forgiven and finally...at peace with everything that has come to pass.

When the constrictions of labels limit us. Sometimes it takes the right person to be strong enough to unravel the stereotypes and wrap us in the right kind of lace.

Playlist

Big Bad Voodoo Daddy - Why Me?

Luis Fonsi feat. Daddy Yankee - Despacito

Imelda May - Johnny Got a Boom Boom

Pedro Capó, Farruko - Calma

Jencarlos Canela feat. Kymani Marley - Bajito

Haley Reinhart - Can't Help Falling In Love

If you get your kicks in a magical manner, order toys from websites like bad dragon, and prefer your monsters *in* your bed instead of *under* them, then Y. D. is your girl.

Writing everything from spicy dark fantasy to fluffier-than-a-cool-marshmallow romance, Y.D. La Mar has her fingers in all sorts of man-meat pie, and the sky is the limit. Somehow, this magical mistress manages to balance her spicy author life with her responsibilities as a mom, a wife, and a resident of Sin City—*oh, irony, you've felled me.*

When the world is full of black-and-white, Y.D. plays in the grey zones, spending her time creating new ways to shock and awe her editor, as well as her readers.

Follow Me!

Want updates and sneak peeks?

Sign up for my newsletter!

Also by YD La Mar

STREET ARRHYTHMIA TRILOGY

The Scent of Jasmine

For The Love of Import & Blood

To The Beat of The Streets

Spinoff

Arachnophilia

REVERSE HAREM

Warring Suns

SCI FI

The Essence of Esme

PARANORMAL

The Hunger of Thieves

Heart of The Reaper

Heart of the Reaper: Tales from the Underworld

Soul of The Reaper

Fate of The Reaper

Bury Me Alive

Lead Me Through The Fire

PSYCHOLOGICAL THRILLER

The Truth Enslaved

CONTEMPORARY

The Formation of Us

The Conception of Us

The Revelation of Us

The House of Eden (cowrite)

When the Bloom Burns (cowrite)

OMEGAVERSE

Gero

Bernhard

Severin

Dystopian/Post Apocalyptic

We Are the Fallen

MONSTER SHORT STORIES

Sinful Attraction

The Sky Below

Maeonia

Between Heaven and Earth

Fantasies Inflamed

Her 13th Hour

Ignus Fatuus

ANTHOLOGIES

Used and Bound

Captured by Darkness

Until the End

After the Rain

Into The Woods

A Foster Fling

Bound by Monsters

Once Upon a Nightmare

Monsters in Love: Lost in the Dark

Monsters in Love: Lost in the Forest

Monsters in Love: Monstrous Ever After

Monsters in Love: Lost in the Deeps

Monsters in Love: Aloha Nui Loa

Pollinators

The Red Key Club: Valentines Day Edition

The Red Key Club: Halloween Edition

Creepy Court

Crimson Vendetta

For the Love of Villains

SHARED WORLDS

Inferno World

Games of the Underworld

Rise of the Dreads

Monsters Ball

Rescue Me: A Hero Romance Collection